# SAVAGE VOW

# WILLOW FOX

Savage Vow

Mafia Marriages Book Three

Willow Fox

Published by Slow Burn Publishing

Cover Design by MiblArt

V2

© 2021

# 1

## KARINA

"Should we really be breaking and entering?" I ask.

My sister, Ivy, is a professional when it comes to party crashing.

I prefer a low-key and simple life. I've never been much of a party girl, but somehow, tonight she's convinced me to join her for a little fun.

"It's not breaking and entering when they leave the door wide open," she touts.

Ivy isn't wrong.

The door is wide open. So is the gate to the prestigious mansion.

But my stomach is tangled in knots.

This is a bad idea.

The worst imaginable, but I follow her.

The girl is trouble, and if she weren't my identical twin and my best friend, I'd have probably ditched her ass years ago.

Funny, being a twin doesn't mean we are anything alike. Sure, we have the same face, great body, and smile, but Ivy is the wild child—I'm the reserved one.

We saunter in through the open door.

The guard standing at the main entrance clears his throat, and with a thick Italian accent asks, "Name?"

The gentleman is wearing a fancy suit and has thick, dark hair atop his head. He's big, like football player size, and could easily toss us out or have us arrested if we aren't careful in what we say.

I open my mouth, but Ivy steps in first.

"You don't know who we are?" She steps closer to the guard, her hand falling to his chest, her finger gliding down his blazer toward his belt. "Zola and Etta Bianchi," Ivy says. She rattles the names off with a confidence that I could never muster.

Ivy must have seen the guest list when flirting with the guard.

I'm trying not to vomit.

There's something about this man that sends a shudder down my spine. We should leave before we end up dead.

His eyes tighten, and he gestures for us to step inside.

She waves to the guard and grabs my arm, tugging me inside to follow.

The house is extravagant. No wonder it's gated with guards. Because of the party, they must have left the gate wide open. The guest list looked extensive.

The music is pounding, and it makes my heart race as Ivy drags me farther into the house. "Are you sure about this?" I ask.

Most of the men are in business suits and aren't speaking English. It's like we stepped into another world, a foreign country, through the front door.

There are women in fancy, sparkling gowns with their hair done up for the occasion. There's no sign of what the party is for. I see no indication of a bride and groom. There are no birthday balloons or banners, although that would seem rather tactless for a function of this magnitude.

It's like a prestigious ball and we're halfway across the ocean. What is the occasion?

The chandelier glistens in the ballroom, and a live band is performing for the guests.

Several women in emerald gowns are walking around with trays of champagne. I grab a flute and down it rather quickly.

The taste is exquisite. Sweet and bubbly, and it tickles my tongue. It's honestly the best sparkling wine I've ever tasted.

Ivy untangles from my arm, and I want to grab her and ask her where the hell she's going when she gives me a reassuring smile. "Relax. Have fun. Drink, dance, make the most of your night off work. You deserve it."

"Where are you going?" I ask.

"I'm going to see if I can find me a hot guy. You should do the same. There are plenty of hotties at the party. Most of them are older too. Yum!"

"Okay," I say. I don't feel the least bit all right or comfortable picking up a random stranger. I've never been a girl to do a one-night stand. But my life isn't exactly conducive to having a relationship, either.

I work a lot, including overtime.

The last boyfriend complained that I didn't spend enough time with him and focused too much on my career. He was four years younger and acted like he just graduated high school.

Exhaling a heavy sigh, I'm glad that Ivy at least convinced me to dress up for tonight. I wasn't sure the party was that extravagant, but I barely fit in with my long black dress with spaghetti straps.

My outfit is simple but elegant. Hopefully, I don't stand out.

I grab another flute of champagne as a woman wanders by, and I accidentally bump into a gentleman behind me.

"I'm sorry." I'm quick to apologize, and it hasn't helped that I've spilled the flute on my gown.

"It's no trouble," he says. He excuses himself from them and grabs a handkerchief from his coat pocket, offering it to me.

"Thank you," I say, dabbing at the spilled remnants of my drink on my wrist and gown. Most of the liquid beads up against my dress, making it easy to clean.

After I finish wiping up my mess, I return his handkerchief to him.

"I don't believe we've met. I'm Aurielo," he says and holds out his hand.

He's handsome, but there's a dangerousness that exudes from his cool exterior. It's probably because he could have me arrested for crashing the party.

Aurielo is several inches taller than I am, his hair short but thick and dark. His eyes are a deep brown with flecks of amber and gold.

One glance at him and he's stolen my breath.

I can't help but wonder what's beneath his suit. He stands tall, thick, muscular.

He's better looking than any guy I've ever dated, not that it matters.

"Etta Bianchi," I lie, giving the name of the guest that we used to sneak into the party. I offer him my hand, expecting him to shake it. Instead, he brings it to his lips.

"It's a pleasure to meet you, Etta." His eyes twinkle as he stares right through me.

The gesture makes me giddy. Maybe it's the champagne that I've had too.

No man has ever paid that type of attention to me. I smile, certain that I'm blushing. The room is several degrees warmer, and one glance past Aurielo and I catch sight of Ivy dancing with another gentleman who is practically twice her age.

Ivy gives me a thumbs-up sign, pleased that I'm mingling.

Goodness, could she be any less obvious?

Thankfully, his back is to her.

"Did you come with a date?" Aurielo asks.

"No," I say. My sister doesn't count. I'm not sure what he's getting at. "Why?"

"Dance with me." He doesn't wait for my answer.

He's not asking.

He's demanding.

He grabs my hand and leads me onto the dance floor.

There's something in the way he carries himself that I find highly attractive, like he knows what he wants and goes for it.

He's not a boy. He's every bit a man.

Aurielo pulls me close as we dance, his hand pressed against the small of my back. His breath tickles my ear when he asks, "What's your real name?"

An unmistakable shiver courses through my body.

"How did you—"

I don't finish my sentence. I want to pull away, run, and make sure Ivy isn't in trouble, but he doesn't let me go. His hold is strong and firm.

"Etta is my ex-girlfriend. You're definitely not that witch," he says with a smirk. "What's your real name?"

"Karina," I whisper as my gaze falls downward.

Shame burns me inside for lying to the stranger. And more so because he saw right through the facade.

He keeps one hand pressed to my back, and the other he lifts my chin to meet his stern gaze. "*Micetta*, do not be embarrassed."

Before I have time to react to his words, his mouth descends onto mine. His hold around me tightens as the kiss deepens.

His touch has stoked a fire burning inside me that he started. He backs me up several feet until I feel the wall at my back.

Aurielo presses himself against me, and his leg pushes up between my thighs, giving me the perfect amount of friction to drive me insane.

Warmth floods through my body.

We shouldn't be doing this. Certainly not in a room full of people.

While I may never see any of them again, doesn't he care what they think?

Music continues to blare through the room, but my mind is in a haze as he ravishes my neck. "Aurielo," I whisper.

He lifts me, my legs wrap around him, and he carries me around the corner and down the hallway. He opens a nearby door and shuts it forcefully, pushing me up against the door.

We're alone.

Just the two of us.

He puts my feet back down on the ground. His hands guide the hem of my dress higher, inch by inch. His touch is rough and commanding, a man on a mission.

Aurielo's eyes bore into mine. "Tell me you want this, *Micetta*." My dress is already hiked up to my waist.

His fingers tease the hem of my black lace panties.

I don't want him to stop.

"*Micetta*?" He whispers against my neck and pulls back to meet my stare.

"Yes," I rasp, my voice barely audible over the pounding of my heart.

He smiles, pleased with my declaration.

"Good girl." He kneels before me and spreads my legs farther apart, inhaling my scent. "*Bellissima*," he says, his voice rough and his hands firm.

He rips my panties right off, and I gasp, surprised by his action and the dominance he wields.

"You're already wet for me."

I slam my eyes shut and revel in the way he makes me feel, the power that he exudes.

His tongue teases and flicks against my pearl. Two fingers caress my entrance before slipping inside. His lips move up my stomach, pushing my gown higher with one hand while the other strokes my insides.

"You're so tight, *Micetta*," he warns. "I don't want to hurt you."

I gasp at his words, his touch, the fact it's been months since I've been with a man. And to be honest, it wasn't anything like this.

He unzips the back of my dress. His fingers slide out, and I whimper in protest.

The smile on his face reassures all concern that I've felt. "Come here, *Micetta*," he says. Aurielo grabs me by the hips and pulls me across the room.

It's an office, and there are papers strewn across the wooden desk. He pushes them to the floor and backs me up against the desk, shaking his head. "I have a better idea," he whispers and guides me around to face the desk.

"Aurielo?" I gasp, naked.

What if someone strolls into the office and finds us in here?

Was there a lock on the door? I didn't notice him locking us in the room.

He bends me over the desk, pressing his hand on my back, my breasts flush with the desk. "What are you —" I begin to ask, but I hear the click of his belt buckle, and then his zipper follows suit.

In one swift motion, he enters me. I gasp and moan. He's big.

Huge.

I gasp as pain and pleasure mix. He's stretching my insides to accommodate him.

He keeps me bent over the table. My body is pressed tightly against the wood as he drives his shaft into me, each thrust bringing me closer to the brink.

I've never been fucked, not like this.

It's raw.

Primal.

And yet still passionate.

My heart races, and my insides clench around him as I begin to tremble.

I gasp and moan, squeezing him, my insides pulsating as an orgasm rips through me.

Aurielo holds on a few seconds longer, grunting, exploding inside of me.

There's a sharp knock on the door. "Aurielo," a man shouts over the music and pounds again on the door.

He's persistent.

Aurielo fixes his slacks and grabs my panties. "These are mine," he says, shoving them into his pocket.

My insides warm at his words, but at the same time, I can't help but worry that someone might discover I'm not wearing any panties. I pull on my dress, and he yanks the door open just as I tug the zipper up.

He doesn't hide the fact that he was with me to the gentleman waiting for him in the hallway.

There's no kiss goodbye.

No exchange of phone numbers or pleasantries.

Aurielo strolls out, and the dark-haired Italian gentleman slaps him on the back, congratulating him.

"Look at you, my brother, getting laid at Nico's engagement party."

I try to sneak out as best I can from the office, but I hear the two men conversing. As I pull the wooden door farther open, it squeaks on its hinges.

"Giovan, chill out." Aurielo casts a glance at me. He gives me a half-cocked smile and nod before dragging his brother in the opposite direction.

I hurry down the hallway and back to the ballroom. It's not a far distance, but my heels tap against the marble floor. There's an elegance to the home that we're in, the kind of place that's rented out for weddings and special occasions. Except, this isn't a mansion that's rented out.

It's owned by someone wealthy. I'm just not sure who or what they do for a living.

Stepping into the ballroom, the music crescendos, and I glance through the throes of partygoers searching for my sister.

Ivy's dark purple gown and yellow trim stand out amongst the crowd. While we are identical twins, we haven't worn the same matching outfit since preschool, when Mom dressed us alike.

I grab another drink from a waitress bringing a round of champagne to the guests. Smoothing down my dress, I feel as though everyone in the room is watching me.

I'm probably overly concerned for no reason.

It's not like they can see that I'm not wearing any panties.

"Ma'am," a gentleman in a dark suit with an earpiece in his ear approaches me. He conveys the look of a guard, but he's not the same gentleman who watched the front entrance.

I press my lips tight together and glance behind me at Ivy. She untangles from the man she's dancing with, but she's cautious about hurrying over toward me.

Does she know something that I don't?

The guard grabs my arm, his grip strong and forceful. "Please, come with me," he says, but his tone isn't the least bit warm or friendly. He's demanding I do what he wants.

I glance once more over my shoulder at Ivy, but she's nowhere in sight.

Did she leave?

Flee?

Is she coming to help me?

"Let go of me," I say and yank my arm from his grasp.

"What are you—"

Before he can finish his sentence, I untangle from his grip and rush through the crowd, back down the hallway that I came from just a few minutes earlier.

The guard's footsteps are thick and heavy as he tromps through the hallway after me.

I should head for the exit, but I'm not sure which way leads out. I sprint down the corridor and whip around the corner to run straight into Aurielo's chest.

Aurielo grabs my forearms to steady me. "Slow down there, *Micetta*," he says.

I glance over my shoulder, gasping for breath. How do I explain that one of the guards is chasing me?

I suspect it's because we snuck into the party, but I'm not entirely one hundred percent confident that's the answer. He seems pissed, and I can't believe it's just because we crashed an engagement party.

"Hold up!" the guard warns as he manages to catch up with me.

Crap.

I glance past Aurielo's shoulder.

Can I make a dash for the door and make it out?

It's about twenty feet behind him.

It's not the front entrance, but I'll happily take any exit that will keep me from ending up arrested for trespassing.

My job has a zero-tolerance policy for breaking the law.

"What's the problem?" Aurielo asks.

I glance up at him. Will he hand me over when he discovers that I wasn't invited?

"Sir, she's not Etta Bianchi."

Aurielo's hold refuses to loosen, his grip tighter than ever.

"You think I don't know that already, Francesco?" Aurielo asks. "Get back to your post. She's with me."

Francesco huffs under his breath and turns on his heel, retreating down the hallway.

"Thank you," I say, relieved that he came to my defense.

Aurielo pulls me silently down the hallway for the door.

He doesn't look at me. His jaw is firm, his shoulders square. There's something he isn't saying. Aurielo unlocks the four deadbolts and grabs the door handle, pulling it wide open.

It seems a bit like overkill, having four deadbolts. Who are these people?

"You need to leave."

# 2

## KARINA

Six Years Later

Everything about the hotel shouts expensive, from the crystal chandelier near the reception desk to the piano player enveloping the room in a warm array of tunes.

My sister has planned the entire night for me as a gift.

Ivy insisted that I take a vacation from my life and responsibilities for one night. On her dime, I was to be thoroughly pampered, with full luxuries of the spa, room service, and anything else that I want.

Ivy is the most thoughtful, sensitive, and protective sister I know, for a girl with a wild party side in her younger days. She's also an amazing aunt to Ashton, my son.

The woman behind the desk hands me the room key and jots down the suite number before giving me directions to the elevator.

I didn't bring much, just an overnight bag and my purse.

The hotel is considerably crowded for early fall.

Maybe there's a convention happening in Chicago this weekend. I don't have the slightest idea. My days are usually spent at work or looking after my little crime fighter, Ashton.

He wants to be a police officer when he gets older.

It's cute, but the idea scares me. He's five, and I'm hoping he'll grow out of it.

I head into the elevator with a few other guests and glance down at the room number scribbled on the envelope for my key card.

I hit the button for the top floor and have to use my card to access the suite from the elevator.

Ivy booked the penthouse suite for me.

I can't even fathom the cost, let alone how she managed to afford it on her measly salary. I love the girl, but she's crazy. It's not like I plan on spending my entire afternoon in the suite.

We stop on two floors before the elevator is empty, and I'm heading up to my suite. I lug my overnight bag over my shoulder and step out into the hallway.

There's only one set of double doors and a black electronic card reader. I swipe my room card, and the lock clicks.

Grabbing the silver handle, I open the door and step inside the suite.

The door slams shut behind me.

The room is enormous, with picturesque windows from floor to ceiling. The curtains are pulled back to reveal the city down below.

I place my bag on the nearby sofa and step around the furniture.

On the floor in front of the couch, is an oversized black duffel bag.

"Ivy?" I call out.

Did she decide to make a surprise visit with Ashton?

The bag is huge for an overnight adventure, but knowing my son, he'd insist on bringing every stuffed animal and truck in his toy box. Bending down, I unzip the duffel.

Male voices permeate the room through the walls.

Someone is in the bedroom, and by the sound of his voice, it's not a young child or my sister.

My stomach flops.

Inside the sack, are dozens of semi-automatic weapons. What the hell did I stumble upon?

I step away from the duffel and grab my overnight satchel from the couch, pulling it over my shoulder.

I don't bother re-zipping the bag. I need to get out before anyone notices my intrusion. I wasn't exactly making myself quiet when I called out for my sister.

The bedroom door is thrown open, and two men with guns point their weapons at me.

"How did you get in here?" the shorter of the two asks. He's got dark, greasy hair and the blackest eyes I've ever seen.

My voice catches in my throat as I try to speak.

"Speak up!" he demands. Stalking nearer to me, he closes the distance between us.

"The hotel must have given me the wrong key," I say.

He's blocking my escape out of the room, and with his gun trained on me, there's nowhere else for me to go.

"We can't have loose ends," a bald gentleman says as he steps out of the bedroom, leaving the door wide open.

There's a younger man with pale skin and copper hair tied to a wooden chair, bound and gagged. He struggles to move, his face bloody, hands bound presumably behind his back.

I walked in on someone being tortured.

The air is sucked right out of my lungs.

I'm going to be sick.

"Aurielo," the bald man shouts.

That name is familiar. It must be a coincidence. Neither of the men with their guns pointed at me answer the bald man.

Aurielo steps out from the bedroom and shuts the door behind himself. There's blood on his crisp white dress shirt and hands.

"Yes, Don Rinaldi," Aurielo says.

My mouth is parched, my throat burns. Tears haven't formed, but I already know what's coming.

I never even had the chance to say goodbye to my son.

"Kill her," Don Rinaldi says.

Aurielo's jaw is firm and tight. He grabs me by the arm, opens the bedroom door, and drags me inside before slamming it shut.

The man tied to a chair is slumped forward. I can't tell if he's dead or not.

"Do you make it a habit of torturing and killing people in hotel rooms?" I shoot at Aurielo.

It's him, the man I slept with, that wild night six years ago. To say that I never thought about him again, would be a lie.

One foolish night landed me pregnant, with a son nine months later. Up until this moment, I hadn't ever fully regretted that decision because it brought me Ashton.

He exhales a heavy sigh through his nose. His piercing amber gaze sends a shiver down my spine as his eyes rake over my body.

"Do you make it a habit of breaking and entering?" he retorts.

# 3

## AURIELO

It's been what, six years since I've least laid eyes on the beauty who stole my heart and nearly got herself into a world of trouble for crashing a party at the compound.

*Karina.*

At least that was the name she gave me that night.

Was it real?

I have no idea.

I didn't try to track her down. It was better that I let her go, escape, set her free, and never think about her again.

Was it fate putting us back on the same path? Bringing us together?

She shouldn't be here, my *Micetta*.

"Do you make it a habit of breaking and entering?" I shoot at her remark about killing people in hotel rooms. She has no idea what she's walked into and how dangerous the situation is for her.

She presses her perfect ruby lips together.

If she's afraid of me, she doesn't show it. I suspect she's terrified but hiding her emotions well. Very few people don't beg for their life when met with the moment of their demise.

"Not my fault the hotel gave me the wrong key," she says.

She's fiery and beautiful. Her looks are pale compared to the personality behind her calm exterior. She's a firecracker. I can see it in those cool baby blues. "Karina," I say, remembering her name from the night we were together.

"You." she opens her mouth and quickly shuts it.

"What was that?" I ask and step closer, closing the distance between us. My hand goes to her throat. I could easily extinguish her life.

She gasps as I touch her, and my hold doesn't tighten.

Choking her is the last thing I want to do to this woman.

Unless it involves foreplay.

"Are you going to kill me?" she whispers, staring up at me.

Challenging me.

I've been ordered to kill her by the mafia boss himself.

Defying an order is suicide. Killing her, I'm not sure that I could live with myself.

At least not yet.

There's too much unfinished business.

I want to discover if she tastes as sweet as I remember and if her body molds perfectly against mine.

If she's dead, I can't do that.

My silence bewilders her.

Karina takes several steps backward and reaches behind herself. She yanks the lamp from the table and pulls the plug right out of the socket, wielding it like a sword.

"Stay back," she shouts.

I smile, trying not to laugh. "My *Micetta*, do you really think you can hurt me?" She's half my size, and while getting hit with a lamp would undoubtedly sting, I'm not concerned that she's going to escape.

"Aurielo," she warns. Her eyes are wide and feral.

"How far do you think you'll get, *Micetta*?" I ask. She's not thinking clearly. "Even if you incapacitate me, there are men outside that door with guns. They'll shoot you before you make it to the front door."

Her eyes flicker.

She knows I'm right.

But she doesn't look defeated. "Then I'll take you as a hostage," she threatens.

It's hard not to laugh at her brashness. She's cute. The pet name I bestowed on Karina fits her even more perfectly than I could have dreamed.

"I have a better suggestion," I say and gesture for her to put the lamp down. The last thing I want is for her to get hurt.

She doesn't lower the lamp, but she does grab the cord with her left hand. Is she planning on strangling me?

"I'm listening."

"Don Rinaldi isn't going to let you leave alive."

"How is that a better suggestion?" Karina scoffs before I can even finish what I intend to tell her. She circles me like I'm her prey.

The girl has no clue who she's dealing with, the power I have, and how close she is to death. Killing her seems wrong, and not because of all the reasons one might consider. She's gorgeous, perfect, all wrapped into one tight little body. Her death would be a real shame.

"Marry me," I say.

She balks at my suggestion. "Marry you? You've got to be kidding me."

It's the only way that I can protect her.

"Alessandro Rinaldi is only going to let you leave one of two ways. Either as my bride or in a body bag."

# 4

## KARINA

It'd be a lie to say that I'd never thought about that party, seeing Aurielo again, or introducing him to his son.

But not like this.

"Alessandro Rinaldi, as in the head of the Rinaldi crime family? You work for the mafia?" I can't hide the terror that forces me into a cold sweat.

I can never let him know that he has a son, that Ashton is his child.

"You will marry me, Karina, and I will protect you." Aurielo steps closer toward me.

I keep a safe distance, as safe as I can, considering the circumstances. I'm practically walking in circles around a bloody guy slumped in a chair with Aurielo closing in on me.

Is the man bound to the chair dead?

I don't see him breathing. I want to reach out, check his pulse, help the man, but I can't do that while defending myself.

"I don't need your protection," I scoff.

Yeah, I could have used that the night we slept together.

But then Ashton wouldn't have been born, and I love my son more than anything in the world. I'd lay my life on the line for him.

"If you want to live, you'll marry me and become part of the Rinaldi family."

I press my lips tight together.

I want to live. I want to see my little boy again, but marrying the monster standing just a few feet away, it's the last thing I want to do.

He's forcing me to marry him.

"And if I say no?"

"Then I'll have to follow the don's orders. I'm giving you an alternative to death."

I'm not afraid of dying, but I am terrified that he'll discover he has a son. Surely, my sister won't know what happened, and if the savage watches my funeral, or worse, attends the event, I can't protect Ashton if I'm dead.

## 5

## AURIELO

"Stay here," I command. "And don't touch anything."

I slip out of the door to have a word with Alessandro.

I may have convinced Karina to marry me, but now I have to convince the boss that this arrangement is favorable for all parties.

"Such a shame a pretty girl had to stumble into our room," Alessandro says. He's going through her bag that she dropped earlier.

I clear my throat and can't help but stare as he shuffles through her belongings, tossing the contents onto the floor. Her black lace panties catch my attention.

Memories of the night we shared together with her pressed up against the office door and desk flood my mind.

"About that," I say. "Might I make a suggestion?"

He drops the empty bag, seemingly disappointed. Did he think Karina was a spy or working with the Feds? If she was, we'd already be surrounded.

"She's not dead yet?"

When I don't confirm his suspicions, he sighs, and his gaze tightens. "Go on," he says and gestures with his hand for me to continue. "There must be something you see in her that I don't if you haven't killed her yet."

The truth is that I know very little about Karina other than her name, her scent, and the way I feel buried inside her body. None of those traits are going to convince Alessandro to keep her alive.

"You have my word that she won't say anything to anyone."

Alessandro folds his arms across his chest. "And what makes you think some two-bit girl is going to keep that kind of promise? The minute she leaves, she'll run to the cops. Your reputation and freedom are on the line," he says.

He isn't wrong.

I'm covered in blood and not just figuratively.

"She'll be just as dirty as the rest of us after I marry her and make her part of the Rinaldi family," I say.

He snorts under his breath. "That I'd like to see," Alessandro says. The corners of his lips quirk upward into a smirk. "I'm not convinced she won't betray you or the family, but when she does, I'll kill you both myself."

## 6

## KARINA

The moment Aurielo steps out of the room to talk to his boss and convince him not to kill me, I rush toward the man bound to the chair in the bedroom.

I feel for a pulse. It's faint but steady.

"What's your name?" I ask.

I want to help him. He's still alive and likely to be tortured to death by the mafia.

He mumbles incoherently.

"I'm going to check your pocket for an I.D.," I say. I try to keep my voice down. I don't want Aurielo to know what I'm up to.

There's no wallet. No form of identification. It's likely already been removed.

"I'll be right back," I say.

I hurry into the adjoining bathroom. It's empty of any bags, possessions, anything that I could use to help the man being held against his will.

I'm not sure what I was expecting to find. I was hoping there were a few prescriptions, something I could have mixed and crushed to at least alleviate his suffering.

There's nothing I can use as a weapon to defend myself.

Returning to the bedroom, I bend down, loosening the man's binds. "I can't find anything to use as a weapon," I say, "but at least you'll have a fighting chance."

I want to believe that he can survive and defend himself, but the men on the other side of the wall have guns.

The bedroom door swings open.

"Get away from him!" Aurielo shouts orders at me. "He's dangerous."

I stand, and Aurielo rushes toward me and yanks me away from the man who is restrained.

I seriously doubt the guy that has been assaulted is going to hurt me.

Aurielo drags me out of the bedroom and into the living room of the penthouse suite.

My bag has been dumped on the floor.

Everything from my panties to my lipstick lies askew.

What were they expecting to find? Was it tit for tat? I searched their bag and discovered their guns, now they ransack my belongings?

"Collect her stuff. Giovan and Francesco, escort Aurielo and the girl to the courthouse for a marriage license. Tomorrow, they'll be wed."

I bend down, and Aurielo helps me gather my belongings, tossing everything into my backpack that I brought for the night.

My purse's contents are buried under my clothes, and I shove everything quickly into my knapsack. The last thing I want is to waste a second and have these men reconsider letting me live.

Aurielo grabs my wallet and flips it open, staring at my identification. Thankfully, I don't have any pictures in my wallet. My phone, however, is a different story. I grab the device on the floor under my pajama bottoms.

He holds out his palm.

Shit.

"I'll take that," he says, nodding toward my phone.

I chew on my bottom lip, and he snatches the phone before I can give him an excuse for why I can't part with the device.

He retrieves his cell phone from his pocket and snaps a photograph of my driver's license. "In case you run," he says. "I know where you live."

Aurielo tosses my wallet at me, and I shove it into my empty purse.

He left the cash in my wallet. There wasn't much.

He's not a thief.

Just a murderer.

# 7

# AURIELO

Don Rinaldi finishes up business at the hotel while Giovan drives Karina and me to the courthouse to obtain a marriage license.

I change shirts in the car and wipe my hands, removing any trace of blood from view.

Francesco waits outside the courthouse with Giovan.

I make sure to leave my gun in the vehicle. Karina isn't carrying a weapon, or she'd have used it on me.

"No funny business," I warn as we walk up the courthouse stairs.

The security checkpoint is just a few feet beyond the glass doors.

My hand falls to the small of her back, keeping her close. I don't trust that she won't run, betray me, or try to escape. While I have her home address, I doubt she'd return there, knowing that we're after her.

She hands her purse to the guard. He glances through it briefly, satisfied that she isn't bringing anything dangerous into the courthouse.

I drop my wallet into a container along with my keys.

Karina steps forward through the metal detectors, and I follow just a few feet behind her. I retrieve my belongings, and she grabs her purse, taking a few quick steps away from me toward the elevator.

Does she think that she can outrun me?

In two strides, I catch up beside her as she steps into the elevator, and I slip my arm between hers, keeping her tight beside me.

"Did you notice what floor we need to go to?" I ask. Since we were already on the ground floor, she doesn't have to worry about catching an elevator going down.

Karina shakes her head no.

I exhale a heavy sigh, and before the double doors close, a police officer steps inside the elevator with us and presses the button marked seven on the elevator panel.

The doors shut.

"Can you tell us what floor we need for the county clerk's office? My fiancée and I are getting married," I say.

"You'll want room 120." The officer smiles at both of us. "And you'll need to head back downstairs." Generously, he presses the button for the first floor for us.

The elevator dings. On his way out of the elevator, he offers us a warm, "Congratulations."

"Thank you," I say and glance at my fiancée.

She gives the police officer a fake smile. He doesn't seem to recognize the look of desperation, but I see it and nudge Karina with my elbow.

"Thanks," she rasps.

Two more gentlemen are riding up the elevator to the twelfth floor before returning to where we started.

I can't help but worry that she'll say something or indicate to them that she's in distress.

My lips tease her ear, lingering against her skin. I make sure that she's not the only one who can hear my whisper. "I will claim you, *Micetta*, every inch of you, on our wedding night."

Her breathing hitches, and I wrap my arms around her, pulling her against me, shoving my lips forcefully on hers.

She tastes just like I remember, sweet, like peaches and cream. Karina even smells just as wonderful, and it takes everything in my power not to lick her neck and undress her in the elevator.

I back her up against the elevator wall, my knee between her thighs, as I trap her against me.

Karina's arms wrap around my neck, keeping me close. She doesn't push me away.

Her lips are warm, and I hear my *Micetta* purr, just like she did that night in the office when I bent her over the desk.

The elevator dings. The doors open, the gentlemen both step off and onto the twelfth floor. When we descend, I release my tight grip and take a firm step back.

A soft blush covers Karina's cheeks. She pushes a strand of hair behind her ear as she avoids my stern gaze.

She did well, better than I anticipated. But I won't say anything, not yet. There are cameras in the elevator as a security measure. Who knows if they're listening in as well.

We reach the first floor, and I adjust my tie.

I'm sweltering inside the elevator—sweat beads at my brow. My stomach is tangled in knots, and I'm not sure if it's because I'm forcing Karina to marry me or the fact that I want her to be my wife.

She didn't object nearly as much as I would have thought.

Karina still hasn't tried to run. Sure, she bolted into the elevator, but that hardly counts. I'm anticipating a chase, a game of cat and mouse, and she's obeying my every command.

I can't fathom why.

We head to the county clerk's office, fill out the required paperwork, show our identification, and are handed over the marriage license.

When we step outside, the autumn air helps cool me down.

Karina's cheeks have returned to a slight blush and aren't nearly as rosy as they'd been earlier in the elevator.

Giovan and Francesco are waiting outside for us.

"Took you long enough," Francesco mutters. He's always been a bit of a grouch.

I wrap my arm around Karina's shoulders. Just in case she decides to flee before we get to the car. "We had a little detour trying to find the county clerk's office," I say.

My younger brother, Giovan, raises an inquisitive eyebrow. He doesn't say anything, but I'm sure a dozen different thoughts are rattling through his brain.

"To the compound?" Francesco asks, as he escorts us back to the vehicle.

"Not yet. I'd like to stop by Karina's place and let her pack a few things to take with her."

"Is that a wise idea?" Giovan asks. He eyes Karina up and down. "She could pack a weapon."

I glance at her as we walk along the sidewalk toward the parking garage. "Do I have to worry about you bringing a weapon?" I fully plan on accompanying her inside her home while she packs.

Her eyes widen, and she appears a bit flustered. "I don't have any guns. Besides, I'm pretty sure you guys have that covered," she says.

I try not to smile at her remark.

Francesco drives us to the address of her apartment. It's on the southside, a rougher neighborhood compared to the location of the compound.

We have a house in Chicago where we also do business, but the compound is in a flourishing, upscale neighborhood north of the city. We own the entire block.

Francesco parks the car, and I climb out with Karina, accompanying her to the front entrance of the apartment building.

She stalls, keys in her hand.

Karina turns around to face me. "If I bring you upstairs, you're going to scare my roommate."

So, she doesn't live alone.

"Is it a male roommate? A boyfriend?" I never bothered to ask if she was seeing anyone or in a relationship. I just assumed when I suggested that we marry that she was single.

"No, just a friend." She chews on her bottom lip.

There's something that she isn't telling me. "I'll wait outside the apartment door," I say, "but you're bringing me inside the building."

She exhales a sigh and gives a brief nod.

Karina seems to accept my proposal.

She unlocks the door, and I follow her into the foyer and up the stairs. "You don't use the elevator?"

"It's broken," she says.

I walk just a few steps behind her, keeping up as we climb eight flights.

Karina is in shape. While I'd noticed her luscious curves, I hadn't realized how she got her work out, just walking up eight flights every time she came home was a chore.

She stalls at the front door, key in hand. "You'll stay here?"

"I will under one condition."

"What's that?" she asks.

"I have to scour your bag and you, to make sure that you aren't bringing a weapon back to the compound."

She seems to accept my proposition.

"All right. Just don't come in. You'll scare my friend."

She unlocks the front door.

"Five minutes," I warn her. "Or I'll break down the door." She slips inside, slamming it shut before I get another word in.

Do I need to worry that she's going to run and sneak out through the fire escape?

# 8

## KARINA

"What are you doing back home early? I paid for a spa day. You ought to be getting pampered right now."

I slam the door shut and lock it.

Not that the deadbolt will do any good if Aurielo breaks down the door. I gesture with two fingers for Ivy to follow me as I hurry into my bedroom.

I rush toward my closet and find the first bag that I can, to stuff clothes inside. It's considerably large and has wheels and a handle for easy navigating.

"I'm in a bind," I say and hold up my hand to silence Ivy. "I stumbled into something I shouldn't have seen, and the mafia is after me."

"What?" Ivy squeals.

I shove my hand over my lips. "Quiet!" I snap at her.

"Aurielo is outside the apartment door, and his men are waiting downstairs for me. If I don't go with them, things will only get worse." I yank open my dresser drawers and start shoving as many of the clothes as I can into the suitcase.

I have to protect Ashton.

"Are you insane?" Ivy asks. "Are you seriously going to go with the mafia?"

What I want doesn't matter.

"They'll kill me, Ivy. I need you to watch Ash until I can figure out how to fix this mess."

Ivy's brow is furrowed, and she stops my hands, resting hers over mine. "We can go on the run, the three of us."

"These men are cold-blooded killers." I grab the zipper, struggling to close the suitcase, tugging on it, but it only budges a few centimeters at a time.

Ivy climbs atop my bag, forcing it shut while I yank the zipper all the way closed. "That's even more reason not to go with them," she says.

I can't take the chance that Aurielo will find out Ashton is his son. "I need you to look after Ashton. You have to be me," I say.

"No!" Ivy shakes her head adamantly. "I can't be you. That's insane. What we did as kids would never work. I can't go to your job. I know nothing about being a pediatric oncology nurse."

I exhale a heavy sigh. I hate it when she's right.

"Okay, then just take care of Ashton. Let him know Mommy loves him."

There's a firm knock on the front door.

"That's him." I drag the suitcase out of my bedroom.

There are toys in the living room, pictures Ash drew on the refrigerator. Evidence of my son. Thankfully, Ashton is at school. I'm not sure that I'd have the courage to walk out if he had been home.

"Coming!" I shout across the room, hoping that Aurielo can hear me through the door.

"Can I contact you?" Ivy asks.

"Aurielo has my phone. I'll reach out to you at work," I say.

Ivy doesn't seem convinced.

She grabs me for a hug and gives me the biggest squeeze that I've ever felt. "I love you. I'm sorry."

Before I can ask why she's sorry, she shoves me hard, knocking me down to the ground. She grabs my bag and slips out the door, taking my place.

# 9

# AURIELO

"I'm ready," Karina says, lugging a massive silver and black suitcase.

"I have to search you," I say, reminding her of our agreement.

Karina scoffs at my suggestion. "The hell you do."

She shoves the suitcase at me to carry her eight flights of stairs. While I intended to take her bag, I didn't plan on the attitude.

"Did you change clothes?" I ask, noticing her in a bright red dress.

I can't remember what the hell she was wearing, but it wasn't that sexy little number. She'd had something much more practical on at the hotel.

"You're observant," she says.

My eyes twitch, and I spin her around and push her up against the wall.

"Ow," she mumbles. "Let go of me, you ogre!"

I spread her legs and keep her pinned between the wall and me.

"That's not part of the deal," I say into her ear. "You assured me that if I wasn't coming into the apartment, I could thoroughly search you, and I intend to do just that," I say.

While I don't have to run my fingers along her bare legs, I take the opportunity to frisk every inch of her thoroughly.

"Search me for what? I'm barely wearing anything," she retorts.

Isn't that the point of why she changed? Why else did she slip into a dress that's suggestive and revealing unless she's trying to hide something from me?

My fingers roam up her thighs, pushing the hem of her skirt higher to ensure that she isn't hiding a knife or any other form of weapon under her clothes.

"Get off me, you pervert!" She slaps my hand away.

I spin her around, her back still pinned to the wall.

She wasn't like this in the elevator, pressed against my body, fighting me. She'd willingly kissed me.

What changed?

Was it all an act because there had been others watching and she was afraid?

"In case you've forgotten, I'm saving your life," I remind her.

"Yeah, right," she snorts. "Kidnapping me and dragging me from my home isn't saving my life. You're ruining it, you mafia monster."

I stare into her blue eyes. There are flecks of emerald that I hadn't seen earlier.

Something isn't quite right, but I can't quite put my finger on it.

I don't trust her.

"We're going inside, and I'm strip-searching you." I can't bring her into the compound brandishing a weapon and risking Don Rinaldi's life.

We'll both end up dead.

"Get your grimy paws off me!"

I snatch her keys from her hands and keep her close against me while I unlock the front door. I don't trust that she won't run.

Just as I unlock the front door, the handle turns before I have a chance to open it.

The front door is thrust open, and those deep baby blues stare back at me.

They're twins?

Karina is wearing a long ivory sweater and leggings. There's a smear of blood on her shirt that I hadn't noticed earlier.

Thankfully, the officer at the courthouse didn't see it, either.

"Karina?" I say.

I glance from Karina to the girl shoved between us, befuddled.

They could have royally fucked with me.

She certainly tried.

Karina steps out into the hallway around her sister. "Please leave my sister out of this. She was just trying to help me."

Grabbing Karina by the arm, I leave her sister at the front door. She's not my responsibility to deal with, and I don't need two of them causing me trouble.

"Say goodbye." I lug Karina's suitcase in one hand for the stairwell. "Francesco and Giovan are waiting for us."

Behind me, the girls exchange a brief hug.

I don't listen to whatever few words are exchanged. It's not my place to eavesdrop, but I make sure they don't switch clothes or try other asinine tactics to trip me up.

A moment later, Karina accompanies me down the stairs.

"Are you mad?" Karina asks. She walks beside me, keeping up with my pace.

"You made me look like a fool. There will be repercussions," I warn. She can't expect to humiliate me and not have to deal with the consequences.

I place the hand on the small of her back and feel her shudder.

# 10

## KARINA

His touch is like lightning against my skin. Aurielo's hand on the small of my back sends warm tingles throughout my body.

I haven't slept with another man since him.

My son has kept me busy, and the thought of dating anyone hasn't surfaced until now.

If I'm to wed Aurielo, I will probably never be on another date again.

"What'd you pack, bricks?" he mutters as we reach the final steps onto the main floor.

"I have to use something to defend myself," I quip.

His eyes tighten, and he stops walking once we reach the landing. He drops the bag to the floor with a loud thud. Aurielo bends down and unzips my suitcase.

"Seriously?" I can't believe he's going to search my luggage now, after carrying it down eight flights of stairs.

He fumbles through a bunch of t-shirts, jeans, pajamas, nothing of interest to him. He lifts my black and purple see-through lace bra in his hand and inspects it with a smug grin. "Did you pack this for me?"

I jab him in the shoulder. "Put my stuff back."

Satisfied that I'm not smuggling weapons into his home, Aurielo shuts my suitcase and zips it back up before grabbing the handle and wheeling it outside.

"About time," Francesco mutters as we approach the vehicle. He unlocks the trunk, and Aurielo shoves my suitcase into the back before opening the back door for me to slide into the car.

Wordlessly, I climb into the backseat, and Aurielo slides in beside me.

"The elevator's out, so we had to take the stairs to the eighth floor," Aurielo recants.

I exhale a soft breath, surprised and relieved that he isn't divulging anything else about what happened with my sister, Ivy.

The men talk amongst themselves as I stare out the window while the city passes us by. "Where are we going?" I ask. My voice is soft and timid.

"Home," Aurielo says.

On the right, outside of Aurielo's window, is the lakefront.

We're traveling north, not that I anticipate I'll have an opportunity to escape. Besides, where would I go? I'd always be on the run, constantly looking over my shoulder, worried that he'd find us.

I don't want that life for my son.

He deserves better.

Francesco drives several more miles before he pulls into a gated entrance. The wrought-iron fence towers above with sharp metal spikes, not letting anyone climb in or out.

The entrance has a key panel and a security camera, watching as we enter the premises.

Lush green grass covers the wide-open yard. There are trees in the distance along the fence line, giving the illusion of privacy.

The driver shuts off the engine, and Giovan steps out, opening the back door for Aurielo. He climbs out first, offering his hand for me to step out.

I hesitate for a brief second. "I can climb out on my own," I say, sharper than I intend.

He doesn't need to pretend that we mean something to one another.

Aurielo drops his hand and steps away, letting me step out of the vehicle while he pops the trunk and retrieves my luggage.

"Do you want to carry your bag inside too?" he shoots back.

He's already set the massive suitcase down, the wheels on the ground with the handle extended, but he hasn't let go of the handle.

"I can carry my things inside," I say.

He exhales a heavy sigh through his nose but doesn't hand over my luggage, dragging it over the cobblestone driveway and up the stairs inside the house.

"This is your home?" I glance at Aurielo.

My stomach flops at the memory of the wide-open front door, the music pouring outside that lured Ivy and me inside.

I hesitate at the bottom step of the entrance.

"Yes, I live here, and so do you. Come on," Aurielo says.

Giovan has already unlocked the front door, and Aurielo is lugging my suitcase up the stairs.

Francesco climbs back into the driver's seat and slams the car door. Is he moving the car or going back to the scene of the crime from earlier?

Aurielo glances over his shoulder at me.

He's waiting for me to join him inside.

I don't want to follow Aurielo, but I need to do everything in my power to protect Ashton.

"Nice place," I whisper. My heels click over the marble flooring. The sound echoes through the foyer and down the ominous hallway.

"Come with me," Aurielo says. He lugs my suitcase up the winding staircase.

The house appears to stretch on forever from the hall downstairs.

He pauses halfway up the stairwell. "Karina, are you coming?"

Exhaling a heavy breath, I follow behind him. Everything is familiar from the brief encounter I had years ago, yet it's a faded memory. I never knew my way around the house. I'd have gotten lost trying to escape the brute who had been after me.

Aurielo leads me up the winding stairwell. The wooden banister spirals as we climb up to the second floor and step off at the landing. There's another stairwell that winds higher, but Aurielo heads down the long hallway.

There are dozens of rooms. I'm not sure how I'll find my bedroom from the next beside it. He turns the handle and pushes the door open.

Light filters in through the curtains.

Aurielo lugs my suitcase inside the room and drops it by the dresser beside the double windows. He pulls back the curtains, allowing more light to stream into the bedroom.

"While we will be married, you'll have your own bedroom. This is where you'll sleep."

I'm not sure if he's expecting a thank you for giving me a separate room, but I don't respond. What am I supposed to say?

"The drawers and closet should be empty." He yanks open the top wooden dresser drawer; the track sticks, but it's workable.

Inside, the drawer is bare.

Aurielo slides the closet doors open. A few items are stuffed on the top shelf. "I'll have everything removed," he says before shutting the closet doors.

Taking a tentative step, I approach the windowsill, squinting from the bright sunlight. Down below, a massive garden fills the courtyard.

There's no escaping my room to sneak outside.

"The bathroom," Aurielo says as he pulls open the bathroom door and flips on the light. "You should find all the usual amenities that you need. If you require anything else, I'll have you give a list to Francesco, and he can pick up those items at the store."

"I can pick up anything I need after work," I say. It's what I'm accustomed to doing or on my day off.

"Work?" Aurielo shakes his head. "My wife doesn't need to work, and you're not leaving the compound without a bodyguard."

Spinning on my heels, I turn to face him. "Excuse me? Just because I agree to marry you doesn't mean you can destroy my life. I have a job that's important not only to me, but to the people whom I help."

His eyes narrow, and his jaw tightens.

"Is that so, *Micetta*?"

He hasn't even asked me what I do for a living or where I work. I doubt he cares a lick about me.

"You can't keep me locked up in this place like a prisoner." I fold my arms across my chest, glancing him up and down. "I'm sure you leave daily. I have a job too."

He presses his lips tight together. His brow is furrowed. "Tell me what you do that's so important that you wouldn't rather live here and stay safe behind our walls?"

Safe?

What is he talking about?

"I'm a pediatric oncology nurse at a children's hospital downtown," I say. "The kids depend on me as well as the rest of the staff on the unit."

What did he think I would do, stay home, and become a baby-making factory for him? He's insane if he thinks he can keep me cooped up in this place.

A deafening silence fills the bedroom.

Aurielo's jaw is tight, but his gaze hasn't left mine. "Francesco can accompany you to work."

"The hell he can," I seethe. "I'm a grown woman, in case you've forgotten. I don't do need your bodyguard babysitting me."

He flinches for a brief second before stepping closer, invading my personal space. "You will bring Francesco to work every damn day."

My hands drop to my sides. "He can wait in the hospital lobby," I say. "My supervisor is never going to let him onto the pediatric ward."

"Fine, but he will accompany you daily to and from work. If you decide to have lunch outside the building, he'll join you." Aurielo towers above me. The heat of his words burn my cheeks.

"Why do you think I need a bodyguard?" I ask. I can't imagine he's worried about my well-being. "Do you not trust that I won't run away from you?"

He scoffs under his breath. "Your sister already tried taking your place. Trust is an important part of a relationship, and to be blunt, no, *Micetta,* I do not trust you."

## 11

## AURIELO

"Trust?" Karina throws her head back and laughs. "We're not really in a relationship. You've forced me into marrying you."

"It was that or I kill you," I remind her. "I don't defy the don."

"Well, maybe you should," she snaps. "Try thinking for yourself for once instead of doing what someone else tells you to do."

She makes my blood boil. My heart thrums against my chest. The beat is hard and rough.

Staring down at her, she's within my grasp, and her scent is intoxicating.

Like that one night I had her bent over the desk, I want her. There's a fire behind her gaze, and it makes my body react.

I reach for her neck, pulling her closer, my fingers tangling in her hair, roughly guiding her lips toward mine.

But I don't kiss her.

I want to rip her clothes off, toss her onto the bed, and lick every inch of her skin, teasing her before letting her climax.

She takes a sharp breath as she inhales.

Karina holds her breath.

Has she forgotten how to breathe?

"You are mine, *Micetta*. You will do as I command, and you will learn to watch your tongue and your tone."

"Or what?"

She's daring me.

Just because we'll be married doesn't mean she's mine to have.

Even if I want her.

And I do—more than anything in the world.

"Or I'll be forced to punish you."

She raises an eyebrow. "What might that entail?" Her breath catches in her throat.

Is she trying to give me a heart attack?

My cock stirs in my trousers at her tone and her question.

It wasn't supposed to be a seductive threat, but damn, she has a way of turning the tables. "You'll be forced to spend day after day in this room, alone. A guard will be posted outside your bedroom door if you can't do as you're told."

Her smile vanishes. "I still have work."

"And Francesco will accompany you to and from work, but there will be no exploring the garden, having dinner in the dining room, or reading in the library if you can't behave. On weekends, the two of us could venture out together if Francesco reports back to me that you aren't causing him grief."

"You're a real joy kill. Do you know that?"

I'm not trying to steal her freedom. All I want is to protect her, not that she understands what we are faced with outside the compound.

"So, I've been told," I say with a shrug. I don't have to explain myself to her. I take a step back and exhale a sharp breath, heading for the door. "Do you want a tour of the house or not?" I shoot at her over my shoulder.

She's exhausting to be around. Is this what I get to look forward to with her?

Karina is quick to follow me out of the bedroom. She's practically on my heel as I accompany her downstairs. I give her a brief tour, revealing the rooms she needs to be familiar with, like the kitchen and dining room.

"What about the garden?" she asks as we breeze past the office.

I lead her down the opposite direction and around the building to the double doors inside that lead to the garden.

"I would never have pegged you men for the garden type," Karina says.

"Where do you think we procure poisons from?"

She doesn't smile or laugh. Karina probably isn't sure whether I'm joking or not with her.

I offer her a grin. "Don't worry, most of it is safe, and everything in the vegetable garden is edible."

Opening the glass doors, I let her outside into the garden. "You are free to visit here whenever you'd like," I say. "But if you want to leave the grounds and go outside beyond these four walls, you will need to take Francesco, myself, or another guard with you at all times."

"Why?" Karina slips off her heels and steps barefoot onto the lush green grass.

"We have a lot of enemies," I say. That's the only explanation that she's getting. "Do you like it out here?" I attempt to steer the conversation back to her.

She strolls farther into the garden, through opening of the small border fence and across the steppingstones. Inside, there's a wooden swing, and she takes a seat on the bench, pushing her feet against the grass, letting the bench glide through the air.

I don't have to ask if she likes it. The faint smile across her features lights up her face.

"Do you come out here often?" Karina asks.

I've never known anyone quite so curious who wasn't a rat in our business. She doesn't strike me as the betrayal type, but I haven't known her for very long.

One day.

"Hardly ever," I confess. "It's too quiet."

"You don't strike me as the meditative type."

She isn't wrong.

"Come sit with me," she says. "The view from here is beautiful. You might like it."

There's a waterfall behind the shrubbery. I can hear the stream of water, but from the path, I can't see much except for her.

"Please," she says with the sweetest voice that makes my heart melt.

"Fine."

I stomp through the grass and cross over the stones.

Karina slows the swing to a halt, and I plop down beside her, the swing wobbling for a brief second. She gets the momentum going again, and my back rests against the wooden slats of the bench, finding it slightly relaxing.

Not that I admit it to her.

"Beautiful, isn't it?" she says, staring at the mermaid fountain.

I have no clue who picked out the décor or designed the garden. It's rare anyone ever uses the courtyard except to woo a lady on occasion.

"It's something," I mutter under my breath.

"You're grumpy," she muses, casting a wayward glance at me.

I give a mere shrug.

So what if I am?

Karina exhales a loud sigh. "If we're going to be married, I feel like I should know something about you."

Again, she isn't wrong. But I don't open myself up to just anyone. Wife or not, no one said the arrangement meant that we had to sleep together.

Not that we haven't already done that before.

"What do you do for a living?" she asks. "I mean other than kill people." A nervous laugh escapes past her lips.

While I'm not a hitman, I've killed more than my share of men. Usually, those men have information to give but refuse to speak. "I'm an interrogator for the Rinaldi family," I say.

She presses her lips together. "Interrogator? That's what you were doing to that guy in the hotel room?"

I clear my throat. Karina asks a lot of questions, more than I'm comfortable answering.

While I already know she works as a nurse, I don't know what brought her to that profession. However, she could ask the same of me. Maybe steering clear of our current jobs would be best.

"You have a twin sister."

"That's not a question," she points out. The swing glides effortlessly and I realize the movement is helping me relax.

"You interrupted me before I could ask a question," I say.

"Go ahead." She gestures with her hands for me to continue.

"What's it like having a twin sister? Do you two live together?" I didn't expect what happened earlier when we went to pick up her belongings.

A faint smile tugs at the corners of her lips. She catches me staring, and her cheeks blush. "Ivy and I may look alike, but we are complete opposites. Sometimes the only thing I think we have in common is our looks and our parents."

"That's two things," I point out.

She laughs under her breath and shrugs. "Yeah, I guess it is. And yes, she lives with me. She helps me around the house, earns her keep since she's a party girl."

"That explains Nico's engagement party."

"Oh my gosh, you remember that?" Her cheeks turn even redder.

How could I not remember that night?

"Yes," I say with a wry grin. "I remember every second of it." I can't help but glance her up and down.

She covers her face with her hand.

"Don't be shy, *Micetta*," I say, reaching for her hand and bringing it down to her lap. "I like it when you blush."

Her cheeks burn brighter on my confession.

"I don't make it a habit of showing up at parties uninvited," Karina says. She chews her bottom lip between her teeth as she speaks. "Ivy talked me into joining her and that, what we did, it isn't like me."

Memories of that night, my fingers pushing her dress higher, flit through my head. "No judgment from me." I enjoyed every minute of her writhing beneath me.

She struggles to meet my stare. "Do you have any siblings?" she asks, trying to change the subject.

"You've met him, Giovan," I say.

Her eyes widen as the realization dawns on her who my brother is since she already met him. "Oh, I didn't realize you were related."

"He's a few years younger but just as protective as a big brother." I glance from Karina to the water fountain. The water glistens under the sun. It's calming to watch. Peaceful.

"Do you want to invite your sister to the courthouse tomorrow when we get married?"

"That's not a good idea," she says.

"Worried she might trick me into marrying her?" I quip, shooting a glance at her.

"I'm sorry about that," Karina apologizes. "I didn't expect Ivy to knock my ass to the floor and take my place."

I cringe at her remark, and my hands bunch into fists at the memory of my hands on her sister. "She hurt you?" I shift on the swing, facing Karina.

How could I have thought Ivy was Karina? Her mouthiness and sass weren't the least bit like Karina's. Sure, she has a mouth on her, but there's a noticeable difference in the way they hold themselves.

"It wasn't on purpose," she says, defending her sister. "Ivy was trying to protect me."

"Protecting doesn't equate to hurting," I seethe. Glancing her over, I don't see any telltale signs of injury. Until she told me, I had no idea what had transpired between the two of them. "Did she leave any bruises?"

Karina quirks a grin. "I haven't checked my ass out in the mirror, but I'm sure it's fine. For a brute like you, I'm surprised you care."

"Brute?"

Is that what she thinks of me?

She reaches for my chest and pats her hand against my suit coat. "I meant it as a compliment," she says.

Karina isn't the least bit afraid of me.

I want to pull her against me, bring her into my lap, and press my lips tight against hers.

But she deserves better. Karina has no idea of the atrocities I've committed. She's only seen a glimpse at the hotel. The whole picture would destroy her.

I'm a monster.

# 12

# KARINA

"Are you planning on following me into the bathroom too?" I ask.

Francesco is on my heels, escorting me from the parking garage into the hospital. "I do what I have to for the job," he says.

"Aurielo already told you, I can't have you following me onto the floor with the patients. You have to wait in the lobby."

He snorts, unsatisfied, but as we enter the hallway and approach the lobby, he grunts.

"If you plan on leaving, you come and get me. I'll take you to lunch or home when you're done," he says.

I have half a mind to leave his ass and escape, but they know where I live, and if Francesco or Alessandro show up at my house, they might not realize Ivy is my sister. And I don't want them meeting Ashton or getting wind that I have a son.

"Fine. You will be my first phone call. Oh right, I don't have a phone."

Francesco rolls his eyes. "Aren't you going to be late?"

Is he trying to get rid of me?

"Just stay. Okay? No causing any trouble, and don't tell anyone that you know me." I don't need more problems following me around.

"Got it." Francesco sits and reaches for a nearby newspaper on a side table.

I hurry to the elevator and hit the button for the pediatric unit. In a matter of minutes, I'm upstairs getting changed into scrubs and tennis shoes at my locker and rushing down to the nurses' station to start my day.

I trip over my feet but right myself at the desk before landing face-first on the floor.

Jocelyn, a fellow nurse and one of my best friends, glances at me. I don't have to say anything for her to know I'm going through hell. Our friendship has solidified over the years through the difficulties of the job.

It's never easy when a patient dies or sitting with the grieving parents, especially when that patient is a child.

"You look like you just ran here from your apartment. And you're late. Is everything okay?" Jocelyn asks.

I had already phoned the hospital that I'd be late for my shift because of an appointment. I didn't elaborate that it was because I was getting married.

Jocelyn's eyes widen, and she grabs my left hand, bringing my ring finger to her face. "You got married and didn't invite me? Girl, you know we can't wear jewelry on the shift."

"I forgot."

"To invite me or take off the diamond? I bet that thing is heavy," Jocelyn says.

She isn't wrong. It is heavy, but mostly it's the emotional weight more than the actual giant diamond ring.

"Walk with me," Jocelyn says and gestures for us to head back to drop off the ring in the locker.

"There isn't much to say."

I'm bad at lying, especially to my best friend.

Her green eyes tighten. Jocelyn glances over her shoulder. "Are you worried about someone else overhearing? It's me you're talking to."

I've never lied to Jocelyn. Not even when I was pregnant with Ashton. She was one of the first people I told my secret to, but not this time.

Telling her might put her life in danger.

It's not like I went on a trip to Vegas and married a handsome stranger.

The man I married works for the mafia.

And he's an interrogator.

I don't want to be on the other side of his wrath.

"I met a guy. We got married. Sorry to disappoint, but there isn't anything more to the story."

I breeze into the back room, fumble with my locker, and shove the ring into my jeans pocket for safekeeping. I shut the metal door with a loud thud.

"Can I borrow your cell phone for a few minutes? I lost mine."

It's a little white lie.

"You lost your phone? You don't misplace anything. Ever." Jocelyn stares at me, waiting for me to elaborate.

"What can I say? Married life is trying." I stalk across the small space to her locker. "Can I use your phone?"

The lockers don't actually lock, and she gives a weak nod. "Go ahead."

I open her locker and grab her phone, unlocking it with her birthday as the passcode.

"Don't take too long. The dragon will be wondering where you are, and I can only cover for you for so long."

"Thanks," I say. I dial my sister's cell phone but wait until Jocelyn is out of the room and the door shut behind her before hitting the green call button.

"Hello?" Ivy's voice resonates through the line.

She wouldn't recognize Jocelyn's number.

"Ivy, it's Karina," I say.

There's a loud rumbling and clanking of pots and pans in the background. "Where the hell are you? Are you okay?"

"I'm fine. I'm at work. Are you all right?"

"Yeah, Ashton is just trying to help me cook lunch," Ivy says.

It's the middle of the week. What is Ashton doing at home? He should be in school today.

"Why isn't he in school?" I ask.

"Parent-teacher conference day," Ivy answers. "Don't worry. I have it covered."

I breathe a sigh of relief. At least Ashton is safe and in good hands with Ivy. "Thank you."

My sister might like to party and be a bit of a wild child, but she recognizes what's important—family.

"Listen, I want to see Ashton. Can you bring him by the hospital and up to the pediatric wing?"

"Are you sure that's such a good idea? What if that ogre is watching you?" Ivy asks.

I pinch the bridge of my nose. I shouldn't be defending Aurielo, but he's not an ogre. "He doesn't have eyes on me all the time." If he did, I wouldn't have been able to make the phone call to my sister.

Which is enough proof that she can sneak Ashton upstairs in the elevator for a few minutes together.

"Okay, but we're making lunch right now. Do you get off work at three?" Ivy asks.

"No, I promised to cover the next shift since I came in late."

"Lucky you."

Yeah, I don't feel the least bit lucky. I have a twelve-hour workday on my feet after a wedding that wasn't the least bit romantic or fueled by love.

"I'll swing by with dinner," Ivy says. "And I'll get you a burner phone."

"You're the best. Oh, and one more thing. You're going to have to use the side elevator near the emergency room department."

"Why?"

"One of Aurielo's men, a bodyguard, is staking out the lobby. If he sees you enter the building, he'll think you're me."

"He doesn't know you're a twin?" Ivy asks with a laugh. "Even after the switcheroo?"

A faint smile tugs at the corner of my lips. "Aurielo didn't tell his buddies about what happened."

"Of course, he didn't. Yeah, we can come in by the emergency room and take that elevator up to your floor."

"Thank you." I hang up the phone and shove the device back into Jocelyn's locker before heading out onto the floor.

I'm already four hours behind, and I swear I can hear the dragon breathing through her nostrils.

———

The day drags on, and I'm relieved when I glance up at the nurses' station, and Ashton is clutching his well-loved bear.

"Mommy!" Ashton squeals, running toward me.

I had already changed scrubs thanks to a toddler vomiting on me twenty minutes ago, so at least my clothes are clean when Ashton embraces me.

I hug him back, holding him tight against my chest. "I missed you so much," I whisper.

It's only been one day.

A lifetime without my son is a nightmare.

"I brought pot roast," Ivy says, revealing the large plasticware container.

"Thank you." I stand, grabbing Ashton's hand as I lead them to the breakroom for a little family dinner.

Jocelyn's already left for the day, or I'd invite her to join us.

Slipping into the breakroom, I hit the lights and grab plastic plates and silverware to dine. There is so much that I want to tell my sister, but I can't with Ashton in the room.

"How's work?" Ivy asks. She opens the container of pot roast. She unzips her oversized purse and reveals a pre-made bag of salad, dressing included.

"Busy," I say. I open the refrigerator stocked with drinks that I had Jocelyn grab from the cafeteria earlier in the day. I pull out two sodas and a container of milk for Ashton.

"How was the parent-teacher conference?" I ask.

Ivy shrugs. "Fine. Ashton plays well with others, colors in the lines, that sort of thing." She waves dismissively.

Is there something that she's not telling me?

Ashton sits at the table, sipping his milk while she dishes out his dinner onto his plate for him.

He's quiet. Quieter than I've probably ever seen him before.

"Ashton?" I hand him a fork and napkin and finally sit down to eat.

He plays with the fork, pushing his food around on the plate. "Eric pushed me on the playground."

"What?" I gape at Ivy. "And you weren't going to tell me he's being bullied?"

"It's not that big of a deal. Boys play rough. Do you remember all the times the boys chased us and pulled our pigtails?"

I can't believe how easily she's dismissing what happened. "What did Mrs. Brown say?" I ask.

"His teacher? Oh, she said that Eric needs to use his words instead of his fists but that she would keep an eye on the boys, and if it continued, then we could arrange for a meeting with Eric's parents."

"If it continues? What's next? She's going to victim blame?"

Ivy pops the tab on her soda, opening it before having a sip. "It's not that big of a deal. Ashton is small for his size, so the kids call him half-pint."

"I'm calling the school first thing tomorrow."

"Don't," Ashton says, his voice timid. "You'll only make it worse, Mom."

I exhale a heavy sigh and mentally count to three. I should count to ten, but I can't make it that far. My patience is wearing thin.

"It's already been handled," Ivy says. "I wish you'd trust me."

Dragon lady, with her gray and black hair and dark brown eyes, steps into the breakroom. "You have a visitor," she rasps. Her voice is thick and rough from one too many cigarettes. Not that Jocelyn or I have ever seen her smoke.

Behind her, Francesco reveals himself from around the corner of the hallway.

"There's two of you? Fuck me," he mutters, catching sight of Ivy seated across from me.

"Mommy, what does fuck mean?" Ashton asks.

My eyes widen, and I stand, preparing to pull Francesco aside and away from the breakroom. The agreement was that he was supposed to wait in the lobby.

Maybe he didn't catch which one of us Ashton was speaking to.

"Mommy?" Francesco repeats the words as I yank him by the arm and drag him away from the breakroom and my son. "You have a kid?" His eyes widen.

Crap.

"You are supposed to be waiting in the lobby," I say and point toward the elevator down the hallway.

Why the hell did the dragon let him stomp through the floor with patients nearby?

"It's been eight hours. You should be done work."

I snort at his justification for checking up on me. "I showed up late for my shift, so I ended up covering my shift and the next one. They're understaffed."

His eyes flinch. "Whose kid is that?" Francesco points toward the breakroom. "He called you Mommy."

"My sister and I look alike. The kid can't tell us apart." I hope my lie slips by without incident.

Francesco doesn't look convinced. "Is that so? You honestly believe the kid can't tell his mother and his aunt apart?"

I bite my tongue and refrain from pointing out that Aurielo hadn't been able to tell the two of us apart.

"What time do you get off your shift?" Francesco asks, his voice gruff.

"My shift ends at eleven o'clock," I say. "I'll need a few minutes to get dressed, and then I'll meet you downstairs in the lobby."

His eyes narrow as he glances me over from head to toe. "No funny business with your sister. Aurielo expects you to consummate the relationship, and he'll know if it's not you he's fucking."

# 13

## AURIELO

My heart strums against my chest.

Francesco ought to be heading home with Karina soon.

My cell phone buzzes against my desk, and I answer the caller, surprised to see Francesco's name pop up.

"What's up? Everything okay?" He's the last person I expect to call unless there's a problem.

"Depends on what you consider to be a problem," he says and clears his throat. "I went upstairs to pay Karina a visit, and she was having dinner with her sister."

I pinch the bridge of my nose and hang my head.

"Her twin sister," Francesco says, elaborating as to the reason for the call.

"I already know she has a twin. They're identical," I answer.

It's best if I don't explain how I know. The last thing I want is to be seen as weak by the Rinaldi family.

"Can you not tell them apart?" I ask with a humph, insinuating that he should know the difference between Karina and her sister.

There's a moment of silence that lingers on the line, and I'm not sure whether he isn't answering or he's cut off with some type of interference. He is at the hospital. It's possible reception is poor.

"It's not just the fact she's a twin. There's a child. A boy."

My mouth goes dry.

I reach for my bottled water, twisting the lid, needing a sip like I'm in the desert and I haven't had anything to drink in days.

"Her child or the sister's?" I ask.

"I'm not sure," Francesco reports. "I thought you might want to do a reconnaissance before interrogating your wife."

"I'll get back to you," I say and hang up the phone.

My laptop is open, the desktop filled with multiple windows. None of them matter.

Does she have a kid?

Maybe it's not her kid, and it's her sister's, in which case, her sister's behavior yesterday makes even less sense.

I rub my temples, an impending headache coming on.

I'm no hacker, but I do a basic search engine investigation and type in Karina Cole. Unfortunately, her last name is far too common.

I narrow it down with the current city and filter through a few records and news articles. It doesn't take me long to land on one listing Ashton Cole and his relationship to her.

His date of birth causes my stomach to churn.

He's a little over five years old.

We slept together about six years ago.

It's probably a coincidence.

If she was pregnant with my son, she'd have told me.

I slam the laptop shut and run my hands through my hair. Pushing my chair forcefully back, I stand, needing some air.

I grab my phone and storm out of the office. I circle the hallway at a brisk pace, going around the entire compound twice before thrusting the doors open and stomping into the garden.

I'm not sure why I'm outside, here, in this calm and tranquil place that reminds me of Karina.

Whether he's my biological son or not, Karina has a kid.

The quiet should be calming, but my heart won't stop racing. I tromp over the stones and onto the wooden swing, throwing myself into it with an overzealous amount of force.

The legs lift effortlessly, knocking me backward, the swing tumbling over.

"Fuck!" I scream.

It takes a second for me to stand, my legs up in the air and my back on the ground.

I climb off the swing and leave the deathtrap on its rear.

I won't let my son or any wife of mine get hurt on that monstrosity.

Bending down, I lift my phone from the grass and dial Francesco. "Is Karina still at work?" I ask.

"Yes, she hasn't left the building yet."

"I'll have Giovan drop me off at the hospital," I instruct. "I want you to drive us to her apartment after her shift."

"I take it the boy is hers?"

I won't elaborate that there's a chance he could also be mine.

He's probably not.

It's unlikely.

We had sex one time.

In my office.

But either way, Karina is my wife, which makes the boy mine.

"Yes," I say. "I need to speak with Alessandro, but I don't foresee an issue with bringing the child to live with his mother."

"Good luck," Francesco mutters under his breath.

I end the call, leave the wooden swing on its back, and head in to have a word with Alessandro. He's easy to find, in his office with my brother, Giovan.

The door is open to his office. "Don Rinaldi, may I have a word with you?"

He gestures me inside. "What brings you in? Is that girl already causing you trouble? I swear she's making you gray." Alessandro cracks a wry grin. "What can I do for you?"

"It's come to my attention, Sir, that the young woman, my wife, has a child."

Alessandro's smile falters, and his face goes grim. "Is that so?"

"Yes."

"And you, what? Want to let her out of the deal that was made? In case you've forgotten, Aurielo, you married her this morning." Alessandro folds his hands together on his desk. "We Rinaldis don't believe in divorce."

"I have no intention of disavowing our marriage. I'd like to provide a room for the child. Separating a mother from her child seems unusually cruel."

"Like you haven't killed men for less?" Alessandro's wry grin reappears. "By all means, bring the boy into the house, but I'm not going to spare another room for the child. If he requires a separate bed, she can sleep with you and give up her bed for him. That shouldn't be a problem. Right? You *are* newlyweds. You should be thrilled to have your paws all over one another."

Alessandro seems overly ecstatic about this new arrangement, which makes my stomach flop.

I wasn't planning on bringing Karina into my bedroom.

I like my sleep.

And hogging all the covers at night.

I intended the marriage to be a sham. Sure, we are wed, but we don't have to sleep together. We will be one of those couples who live separate lives, under the same roof.

"You're dismissed," Alessandro says when I don't respond to his remarks.

I retreat from his office, foregoing asking Giovan for a ride to the hospital. Taking my vehicle is pointless since Francesco will insist on accompanying us.

He's as much a bodyguard for her as a spy for Alessandro. It's doubtful he'll let her out of his sight.

I walk out to the main road and grab a cab.

My fingers tremble, and I shove them in my pocket, not wanting to feel the least bit uneasy about what's going to go down.

Will Karina hate me for bringing her son into this life?

She tried to shield him from me.

Why?

Is it because I'm a beast?

She's barely witnessed that side of me and the monster that gets unleashed. It only surfaces when interrogating a suspect or when I'm given orders to execute.

## 14

## KARINA

I have half a mind to bolt. Francesco is expecting me any minute downstairs, and if I don't hurry, he'll come looking for me.

I finish changing out of my scrubs and slip my wedding band back onto my ring finger.

The weight of it is heavy.

A grim reminder of my commitment to Aurielo.

"Night, Karina," one of the staff members says as I head for the elevator.

"Bye," I say and give a brief wave before riding the elevator down.

Francesco is waiting for me in the lobby.

But he's not alone.

He's standing speaking with Aurielo.

Why is he here?

I press my lips tight and stride toward the lobby. Even if I wanted to make a beeline for the exit, Aurielo's already laid eyes on me.

"Done with work?" Aurielo asks. His expression is neutral, and I can't read whether he's upset with me for being at the hospital late or if it has to do with something else.

That something else being my son.

He slides his arm into mine, escorting me to the parking garage where Francesco parked the car earlier in the day.

It's still in the same space.

Aurielo yanks open the back door and gestures for me to get inside the vehicle.

I climb in, and he slams the door.

Goosebumps form on my arms.

He struts around to the opposite side and opens the back door, scooting in to sit beside me.

Why didn't he sit in the front seat beside Francesco?

"We need to have a little talk." His gaze is trained on me.

I shift, uncomfortable with his scrutiny, while Francesco starts the engine of the car. A few seconds later, he's backing us out of the parking space.

"About what?" I don't want to give him any more information than he already has from Francesco.

What did he tell Aurielo?

That I have a nephew or a son?

"Cut the crap, *Micetta*!" His voice reverberates through the car.

I shiver and scoot farther away.

Will he hurt me?

I honestly don't know. He could have killed me and he didn't yesterday, but this is the first time I've seen his face red and been on the receiving end of his shouts.

"Who's child is it?" Aurielo asks. His eyes bore into mine.

Aurielo's stare is unnerving.

I want to climb out of the car and run, but I can't get away.

We're traveling down the parking garage, but more importantly, the doors are child-locked. I should have flipped the switch on the door and taken off the first chance that I got.

"Don't lie to me." He shifts his body, his knees brushing against mine. "Is he my son?"

"No."

It's an easy lie.

Ashton isn't his.

Biologically, he may be the father, but Ashton will never be his son.

He exhales through his nose quite loudly. "Doesn't matter. We're married. Which makes him mine. Just like you belong to me." His eyes flinch and tighten.

I scoff at his notion of marriage. "I'm not a piece of property that you can own."

"No? Your son will come and live with us. A mother shouldn't be separated from her child. Believe it or not, I'm not a monster."

A shiver runs down my spine.

"I'd prefer if he stayed with his aunt," I say, my jaw firm. It takes every ounce of courage to send Ashton away, but it's for his safety. I'm only thinking about what is best for my son.

Ashton doesn't need to grow up in a world of criminals and murderers. He deserves a normal childhood.

"Well, that's too bad. We're heading over to your apartment right now to gather the boy and his belongings," Aurielo says.

"What?" I glance out the window as I realize we're heading south, in the opposite direction of Rinaldi's mansion and picture-perfect home. "No, you can't do that."

"I agree. Traveling into the southside at night is foolish. I can't believe you live here with a child."

Raising a kid isn't cheap or easy, not that Aurielo needs to know about my struggles. I'm not looking for a sugar daddy or a handout. I've done fine on my own, mostly. My sister has been there to help with childcare and shuttling him to and from school recently.

"Not all of us can live in mansions with butlers and sit on a yacht all day soaking up the sun."

"Alessandro doesn't have a butler," Aurielo says. "And quite frankly, I'm insulted you think that our wealth isn't anything but hard-earned."

Hard-earned? He has to be kidding! "Right, selling drugs to school-age kids and weapons to thugs."

"We don't sell to kids. We have morals," Aurielo says. He folds his arms across his chest, apparently taking offense to my comment.

But he doesn't deny the weapons accusation. How could he? I saw the duffel bag filled with guns.

"Morals?" I laugh. He's the least moral person I know. It's not like I hang out with drug dealers and mafia scum regularly.

"I'm not a bad guy," Aurielo says. He's a little too calm and collected.

"You were ordered to execute me. Murdering someone is what, ethically acceptable to you?" I stare him down and don't so much as flinch when I shoot him question after question. "Why? Because I witnessed a crime?"

"Well, when you put it like that," Aurielo says and smirks. "We don't sell guns or drugs to school-age children. You act like I'm the devil."

"Aren't you?" Doesn't he see why I don't want him around my son?

Aurielo leans in. His breath lingers a little too long.

The heat between us sizzles, and I wrap my arms across my chest, hoping that he overlooks my sharp intake of breath or the fact that his proximity affects me.

I don't want it to affect me.

I don't want to feel anything for the cold-hearted murderer.

"In case you've forgotten, I saved your life," Aurielo says.

He doesn't have to remind me. The damned ring on my finger is enough of a reminder.

"You mean forcing me to marry you?" The nerve of him to act like he's so high and mighty when otherwise he'd have killed me.

"I'm regretting that decision every second," he mutters under his breath.

"You and me both."

Francesco pulls up to the apartment complex and shuts off the engine. He opens the car door for me as he stands on the curb.

I stall for a second but finally relent, stepping out.

Aurielo climbs across the backseat, following me to the door.

Is it too much to ask for some privacy? With the two of them, someone is always shadowing me.

Francesco waits by the vehicle while we climb up the stairwell eight flights.

I'm not light in my footsteps, doing all that I can to get my frustration and anger out on the stairs.

"Stomp a little harder," Aurielo comments.

I'm surprised he notices.

Then again, everyone living in the building on the floors we pass probably heard me.

Finally reaching the eighth floor, I approach the door and hesitate. "Are you sure you want a kid at the palace?" I ask. "I mean, won't your boss get annoyed having a little boy running around like a wild beast?"

"First off, the house isn't a palace. It's a fucking compound," he says with a grunt. "Second, you'll be expected to control your child. He's not a free-range animal."

I'm about ready to slap him. "Is that a joke?"

Aurielo cracks a wry grin. "Quit stalling, *Micetta*."

What the hell does *Micetta* even mean? Is it his pet name for me or an insult that he likes to throw at me with every opportunity that presents itself?

"I don't have my house key. I wasn't planning on visiting home."

I give a firm knock.

"What do you want?" Ivy's voice resonates through the door. She probably glanced through the peephole and saw the asshole beside me.

"Let us in," I say.

"Is that you talking or the guy who likes to feel women up?" Ivy quips.

Aurielo shrugs. "I was checking her for a weapon."

I roll my eyes and knock again. Like that will make a difference. "Come on. I don't have my key, and we're going to bring Ash home with us."

"Ash?" Aurielo asks. "Who the hell names their son Ash? That better not be short for Ashley."

Fuck.

Does he ever shut up?

"It's Ashton," I snarl. I'm not all bark and no bite. I'm ready for a throw down with Aurielo. I don't care if he is mafia.

The locks click, and Ivy slowly turns the handle of the front door, inching the door open.

She's hesitating, and I can understand her predicament, but this is my apartment, and Ashton is my son.

"Are you sure about this?" Ivy asks.

I'm not sure, but I can't voice my concerns to Ivy. She'll probably pull a knife on Aurielo, and as tempting as it would be to watch him squirm, I don't know what worse fate would fall on my family or me.

"It's fine." I step in past the foyer and notice the television on and cartoons running in the background.

It's nearing midnight, and Ash is asleep on the couch. I want to chastise Ivy for letting him stay up past his bedtime. He should be in his bed asleep, but she's always been a softie with rules.

"He's been asleep for a while. I didn't have the heart to put him in his room," Ivy says.

I give her a side glance. I don't buy her bullshit. "Right. That's why you're still watching cartoons."

Whenever she's been over at my apartment, the minute Ash is out of the room or asleep, she always turns the channel immediately.

"I'm a softie," Ivy says.

I head into Ashton's bedroom and pull open the closet, retrieving the suitcase buried in the corner.

It's not nearly as fancy as mine with wheels, the zipper sticks, and the corner fabric is fraying and thin, but it will suffice.

I yank open the drawers, cleaning out his clothes, stuffing everything inside the bag.

Aurielo stands in the hallway, watching Ashton sleep from a distance.

"Get in here," I demand. I don't want him spending any time with my kid, alone.

It's late, and I'm spent. I don't want to deal with packing up Ash's toys and clothes. If I forget something important, the kid will have a fit.

Aurielo can help. It's his fault we're here.

"What can I do?" Aurielo asks, his tone more cheerful than I anticipate.

"There's a duffel on the top shelf. Pack his stuffed animals on his bed, some toys from the toy box by the window. I'm sure you don't already have stuff for him to play with, and if he's bored, you'll regret bringing both of us into your home."

Aurielo takes orders like a pro.

I glance over my shoulder as he grabs the stuffed animals on the bed first before sifting through the giant bin labeled *toy box*.

In a matter of minutes, I zip up the bag and let him carry both pieces of luggage while I head out of the bedroom to grab Ashton.

"Are you sure about this?" Ivy asks. Her eyes bore into mine. She has a cell phone in her hand. I glance down and notice the numbers 9-1-1 are already punched in, but she hasn't hit send yet.

She's hesitating, and while I'm not sure why, I'm relieved.

"Everything is fine. Don't worry." I assure Ivy as I gesture for her to put her phone away. "He's not kidnapping me, I promise." I show her my wedding band as if that makes everything all right.

"You're married?" she squeaks, her voice higher than I've ever heard it.

It manages to wake my son.

"Mommy?" Ashton mumbles, rolling around on the sofa.

"I'll tell you about it another day." Thankfully, she brought me a new phone that I can use to text or call her. Not that Aurielo knows, but he'll probably assume that I'll ask to call her. Maybe I will, just so he doesn't realize I have a burner phone.

I stalk toward the sofa and bend down, lifting Ash into my arms.

Instantly, he wraps his arms around my neck, his face burying against my skin as he clings to me.

He's heavy, but there's no way in hell I'm going to let Aurielo carry my son to the car.

I try to hide the struggle, and Ivy opens the front door.

"Let me carry him," Aurielo says.

"No, you're a stranger to him."

He sighs and relents. That's enough of an answer to satisfy him. "Okay, but if you change your mind."

"I won't," I snap back at him.

It's a painful eight flights of stairs carrying Ashton. I'm not weak. I've had to move patients, but carrying a kid who's deadweight down eight flights of stairs is exhausting.

When we finally reach the vehicle, I'm relieved to put him into the backseat. "He needs a booster seat." I glance up at the apartment building as it looms above us.

The last thing I want is to leave my son with these two strangers, and I can't very well carry him back up eight flights and then down another eight.

Aurielo nods as he loads the luggage into the trunk. "Is there one in your car or upstairs in your apartment?"

"It's upstairs," I say. "The spare booster is in Ivy's car, which is locked in the parking garage."

"I'll be back."

I feel bad for Ivy, having to answer the door when Aurielo shows up without Ashton or me. But I'm sure they'll work it out.

I climb into the backseat with Ashton. My neck is sore and throbs. I crack it from side to side and grimace. My shoulders are tight too.

Several minutes later, Aurielo reappears, carrying a booster seat in his right hand.

The backdoor is left wide open, and he bends forward, leaning in to hand it to me.

"Thanks." I secure the booster seat and then put Ashton into the seat before buckling myself into the vehicle.

Aurielo opens the front door and sits up there with the driver.

Relieved he's not scooting in close to my boy, I stare out the side window and try to relax. I'm exhausted. My feet hurt from standing on them all day. My back and neck hurt from carrying Ash down eight flights of stairs, and I don't even get to go home after a long day at work.

My eyes burn with tears, but I don't cry.

Aurielo and Francesco talk amongst themselves in the front. I can't understand a word of what they're saying, because it's not in English.

Italian maybe?

They are mafia.

That would make sense.

I try to relax, but I can't settle down.

My heart races as I glance beside me at Ashton.

This isn't what I want for him.

He deserves better. A mother who doesn't fuck everything up. Not that walking into the hotel yesterday was my fault, but opening that zipped bag sure as hell was my doing.

If I could do it all over again, I'd change the course of events. I'd forego the hotel, massage, spa day, and just stay at home.

But I can't change what happened.

I'm stuck here, married to a man who doesn't love me. He doesn't even know the boy in the backseat is *his* son.

I can't tell him. If I do, he'll never let me leave.

Right now, there's still a chance—a glimmer of hope that he'll let us escape.

## 15

## AURIELO

It's late. I should be tired, but I'm wide awake.

Francesco is driving us home, back to the compound.

*"Did you see the kid?"* I ask Francesco in Italian.

Karina's given no indication that she understands a word of what we've said, and I'm confident if she knew some of the vulgar names I called her to test her understanding, she'd have had a fit.

*"Looks like every other kid,"* Francesco answers, his eyes focused on the road while we drive through the city. It's always crowded and busy. It doesn't matter what time of day or night.

Maybe Francesco didn't get that good of a look at the boy. It's dark outside. I don't fault him for that, but I swear the eyes, the nose, and hair are the spitting image of what I looked like as a kid.

He isn't wrong, though. Kids look alike. Isn't that why babies wear bracelets in the hospital? So, they don't mix up the kids.

*"Why are you asking?"* Francesco glances at me.

*"No reason."*

He snorts, not believing me, but keeps his hands on the wheel and his eyes trained on the road.

Francesco lets us off at the front entrance when we pull up at the house before he parks the car around the back. I climb out of the front seat and open the door for Karina.

Her eyes are weary. I can't tell if it's from a long day or resentment at bringing her son here to live with us.

Probably a bit of both.

She unbuckles a sleeping Ashton from his booster seat and carefully maneuvers him out of the car.

"Let me take him," I offer again, and this time I won't take no for an answer.

He's asleep, and from the sound of him softly snoring, he isn't about to wake up, either.

"You'll be right with me the entire time," I say, assuring her that I do not intend to cause any harm to her son.

I can see the trepidation in her eyes and worry lines crease on her forehead.

"I promise I'll be careful and gentle. Let me do this for you," I say.

All I want to do is help.

We may as well make the best out of the situation that we've been thrust into, even if it was by my hand.

She relents, handing him over. "Careful," she whispers.

Francesco grabs the luggage from the trunk and leaves it by the front entrance.

I carry Ashton inside and up the stairs, with Karina right at my hip.

"He'll need his own room," she whispers, attempting to keep her voice down, but she's terrible at whispering.

I try not to tell her to be quiet, or she'll wake her sleeping son, and neither of us wants that to happen.

"Follow me," I instruct as I head down the hallway to the room that she slept in the previous night. I stop in front of her room, and she gets the hint, opening the door to her bedroom.

Thankfully, Ash is already in his pajamas, making it easy for me to guide him under the covers and tuck him into bed.

It feels strange putting a kid to bed.

Karina kisses him goodnight, and I gesture for her to follow me when she's done.

Her brow furrows, but she relents, her feet soft against the marble flooring as she heads out into the hallway with me. I quietly close the bedroom door behind us.

"Am I sharing a bed with my son?" she asks. "I thought you'd have two rooms for us."

"There are two rooms. One for your little boy and the other for us."

She swallows, and I watch her tug her lip between her teeth. "Us?" her voice croaks.

It's sweet.

Almost endearing.

I'm waiting for her to fight me, insist that she have her own separate bedroom, or threaten to cause me bodily harm. She certainly seems capable.

"Is this your idea of a joke?" She folds her arms across her chest. It's her defensive posture. I've seen it enough times in the past twenty-fours with her that I know when she's pissed.

I tend to piss her off a lot.

"No. I asked Alessandro for an additional room, and he denied the request. Said that we're married, so he expects us to share a bed."

She drops her hands at her sides and steps closer toward me. "I'm not sleeping with you."

"I wasn't asking you to sleep with me, *Micetta*." I'd never force a woman into my bed.

"You can sleep on the floor."

It's more generous an offer than I thought she'd give.

There's a small couch in the bedroom that I could claim, but I'm much too tall to be comfortable, and the marble floor is not generous on my back or knees.

"It's late," I say and grab her wrist, bringing her to follow me to my bedroom.

She shrugs out of my touch. "Just because we're married, I'm not doing *that* with you."

"What's that?" I ask innocently. We're three doors down from Ashton. I'll request to Alessandro again about reassigning a different room to Ashton. Even if he doesn't want to let Karina have her own room, we ought to be closer to the kid. I'm sure that would make Karina a little more comfortable, too.

Her nose scrunches slightly in the most endearing and adorable way possible. "You know. Married stuff."

I open the door to my bedroom, and she gasps.

"Acceptable enough?" I ask.

"It's huge." She strides across the room and glances out the window at the front lawn. There's decorative lighting outdoors that filters in soft light, but when the curtains are closed, they keep the bedroom black as night. "You have four windows."

"It's still smaller than the master suite," I say. Alessandro's room is impressive. Not that she needs to see his bedroom, ever.

She points at the wayward couch in the corner of the room. "You can sleep there."

"Nice try." There is no way I'm sleeping on that damn couch. My legs will be bent over the edge, and my body kinked up.

No. Fucking. Way.

"I'm serious. The couch is your bed."

I don't care how serious she thinks she is. I'm not sleeping on the couch. "You're smaller. You take the couch. Only seems fair." I'm trying to be rational with her. I'm willing to share the bed, but if she doesn't want to join me, then I'm giving her another place to sleep. And I'm generous that it's not the hard marble floor.

She pouts but doesn't budge from her position at the window. "My clothes are in Ashton's bedroom."

I head to my dresser and pull out a t-shirt for her to wear. "You can borrow something of mine to wear to bed or sleep naked."

It's impossible for my eyes not to wander down her body. I want to see her naked, tear her clothes off, explore every inch of her body.

"I'll take a shirt," she says and holds out her hand for me to deposit the clothes into. "And boxers. You don't get to see any part of me naked, ever again."

"Ever is a long time," I mutter under my breath as I yank the bottom drawer open and grab a pair of gray sweatpants with a drawstring.

One night, nearly six years ago, wasn't enough.

But I doubt she'll ever break down the wall that she's built around her heart.

Not that I blame her.

She has a kid.

And I forced her to move in here, marry me, and uproot her life. I'm the bastard in this situation, but I want to make right by her. Karina deserves that much.

It's why I haven't demanded that she quit her job and give up her career. Francesco wasting his day as her bodyguard while she's at work is an inconvenience at best. I'm lucky Alessandro hasn't made the call to get her sacked.

I toss the clothes onto the bed and stalk toward the shower. I'm tired, grumpy, and getting a hard-on just imagining her in my clothes and under the covers of my bed.

I need to get laid.

Which isn't going to happen ever again.

I'm not a man to cheat on my wife. I have principles.

But fuck it, not having sex for the rest of my life is not something I can handle.

Forever is too long.

"Where are you going?" she calls after me. I don't bother with grabbing clothes. There are already clean linens hanging in the bathroom.

"A shower," I mutter and shut the door abruptly to the bathroom.

I can hear something muffled on the opposite side of the door. I don't know what she said, and I don't care enough to find out. She's probably complaining that the accommodations aren't up to her standards.

I flip the fan on in the bathroom to drown out any other sounds she makes. I start the shower and strip down, the unmistakable sign of my arousal impossible to ignore.

I need a cold shower.

But that's not what I want.

I want *her*.

I crave every inch of her body tangled around mine, my cock nestled inside her warmth.

But I won't force myself on her. Married or not, that makes no difference.

I climb into the shower, stand under the icy cold spray, and eventually turn the water too hot, unable to handle the goosebumps forming on my arms.

Karina doesn't have to know I fantasize about her.

She never has to find out.

Finishing in the shower, I dry off and secure the towel low around my waist before opening the bedroom door.

She's curled up under my covers. Her hair is splayed out across the pillow, eyes closed.

There's a hint of a smirk at the corners of her lips, and even in the darkened room with only the glow of the bathroom several feet away, I'm confident she's blushing.

Karina is watching me.

Does she like what she sees?

I stroll toward the dresser, taking my time, dropping my towel, my ass within her view as I open the drawers and fumble around with finding a pair of boxers to wear to bed.

It shouldn't take me this long to pick out something for bed, but I'm listening and can swear I hear her sharp intake of breath.

I'm not mistaken.

Her breathing quickens.

Karina hasn't said a word indicating she's awake, but without a doubt, I know that she's watching me and she's enjoying the show.

Dare I say I've aroused her.

I glance over my shoulder, and she slams her eyes shut.

## 16

### KARINA

I'd almost fallen to sleep, but my mind won't stop racing.

Ashton is going to panic when he wakes up in a strange bed and an unfamiliar place. I should have stayed with him. Even if it meant me sleeping on the floor, he'll need me.

What happens if he stirs in the middle of the night? Or he has a bad dream?

The shower turns off, and Aurielo will be out any minute. He's going to expect to share a bed.

I don't want to, and I've made that clear, but the couch is more like a love seat, and the last thing I want is to end up sleeping on it because I'm the smaller of us.

Maybe I should have put Ashton on the couch and stolen Aurielo's bed. He could have taken over my bedroom, where Ash is sound asleep.

It's too late for that now.

I'm not moving Ash again. He slept soundly on the car ride over. The last thing I want is to wake him and be up the rest of the night.

I need to sleep. I've got work tomorrow and a kid who is going to be panicking in the morning. Not to mention I need to get him to kindergarten, which is across town, and figure out picking him up and dropping him off with my work schedule. Ivy had been helping with that transition, with him going from preschool to kindergarten.

The bathroom door opens, and I shut my eyes. I don't want to converse with Aurielo.

Anything I say at this point will come out sharp, and I'll regret it. I'm exhausted and sore as hell.

His footsteps against the hard marble are soft and gentle. It's uncharacteristic for Aurielo. At least my impression of him. He's tough, a ruthless savage. Aren't all mafia men monsters?

My eyelids flutter open, and he drops the towel, rummaging through his dresser drawer.

The soft light from the bathroom outlines his naked body.

He's beautiful—every inch of him.

Six years ago, I never got to see him naked. We didn't make love. We didn't savor the experience.

It was a quick and dirty fuck.

I'm not complaining. I enjoyed what he offered, but I didn't get to feel over every inch of his skin, taste him, touch him, explore his body.

The room is stuffy, and while I want to push the covers off my body, Aurielo will notice that I'm not asleep.

I've already made the mistake of pretending to be out cold.

I exhale a soft breath, a slight puff of air as I study his body, his muscles, and his exquisite frame. I may never see him like this again.

He glances over his shoulder and catches me staring at him.

Shit.

That was not supposed to happen. I slam my eyes shut and groan. I roll over so that I don't have to face him or my embarrassment.

Aurielo chuckles under his breath. "I knew you were awake."

He's not nearly as quiet as he shuffles his clothes on, then shuts off the bathroom light and strides toward the bed.

"I can't sleep." It's not a lie. It's been exhausting.

Aurielo pulls back the covers and climbs into bed beside me. "I can put a pillow between us if that will make you more comfortable," he offers.

That isn't going to solve the problem of us sharing a bed. "Just keep to your side," I mutter. The room is still sickly hot, and I'm confident my cheeks are burning. I push the covers down, needing a bit more air.

"Okay, not a cuddler. I'll remember that," Aurielo quips.

If this situation weren't quite so awful, I'd find him a bit endearing. But liking him means giving in, and I refuse to grow attached to him or anyone else under this roof other than my son.

My silence must be enough to make him realize I'm tired and ready for bed.

"Goodnight, *Micetta*," he whispers into the darkness.

I don't answer him. This isn't how I imagined I'd be spending my wedding night, married to a man by force to save my life, separated by a pillow, and neither of us wanting to share the same bed.

Well, I don't want to share the bed. I assume he doesn't, either, but he hasn't said either way.

I can't imagine his feelings for me are anything more than pity. That is why he saved my life. Isn't it?

———

I awaken early the next morning and climb out of bed in the darkness.

The room is unfamiliar, but the slight glow from the sunrise peeks in through the edge of the curtains. It offers enough light for me to stumble through the bedroom and retrieve my clothes from the previous day.

Everything of mine is in Ashton's room.

I sneak into the bathroom, change, and run my fingers through my messy tresses before hitting the bathroom light and quietly tiptoeing to the door.

"Where are you going?" Aurielo's voice resonates from the bed.

"Ash will be up soon. I don't want him to wake up alone in an unfamiliar place."

He sighs and rolls onto his back. "Let me make the two of you breakfast this morning."

I catch a glance at him. His hair is disheveled, and the pillow that was nestled between us isn't hiding the man I slept beside.

Aurielo isn't wearing a shirt, and his chest, even in the darkened bedroom, is incredible.

Pressing my lips between my teeth, I try not to stare at him half-naked on the bed.

"You don't have to put yourself out. I'm sure you have work to do." While I appreciate the effort that he's attempting to put in, it isn't necessary.

"I wasn't asking, *Micetta*. I want to meet your son. *Our* son," he says.

My stomach flops.

"Our son?" I croak.

He can't know that Ashton is his child.

I never put his name on the birth certificate.

Only Ivy and Jocelyn know who the father is, and they aren't going to say anything.

"Well, we're married. Which makes him my son."

While I appreciate his concern, Ashton is my child. I've raised him, and for Aurielo to think he can take charge, he's in for a headache.

"Legally, that isn't true." I fold my arms across my chest. "I appreciate what you're trying to do, but Ashton is my son."

"And you're my wife," Aurielo says matter of factly. He throws the covers off and stands, clad only in his boxers.

Did someone turn the air conditioning down? Sweat beads on my forehead. My mouth is parched.

He strides across the floor, coming toe-to-toe with me. "Your son is my son. Our son," he says, correcting himself. "And while that might not legally be the case, we can easily rectify that situation."

"No," I whisper, staring up at him. He may be chained to me through the binds of marriage, but I'm not letting him get his claws into my child. When I find a way to escape, I don't want him demanding custody of Ashton.

He can't ever find out my son is his biological child.

Aurielo reaches out, his hand lifting my chin to meet his stare. "No one defies me, *Micetta*."

"I'm not your prisoner or your lover," I remind him.

Except I'm exactly that, a prisoner. Bound to him so that I will survive.

His gaze tightens, and he drops his hold on me. "Go be with your son."

Aurielo opens the bedroom door, and I dash out of the bedroom and into the hallway, rushing to Ashton's bedroom door.

There's a guard posted outside, but he doesn't pay me any attention. Did Aurielo or Alessandro request the guard to be stationed outside Ashton's door?

With ease, I turn the handle on the door and sneak into the bedroom.

I'm light on my feet, careful not to wake Ash.

In the corner of the room, is an oversized plush chair. I take a seat, but it isn't long before Ash begins to stir.

"Hey, sweetie. Mommy's right here," I say and stand, coming to sit at the edge of the mattress. "How did you sleep?"

His gaze darts around the bedroom. "Where are we?" he asks, ignoring my question as he sits up in bed.

How am I going to explain this to him?

## 17

# AURIELO

The kid looks exactly like I did when I was five. Well, maybe not exactly. But the resemblance is uncanny. Light brown hair, long, thick eyelashes, a small button nose, and thin delicate lips.

It's a coincidence. Right?

He's not my son.

Karina would have told me that I have a kid. She'd have come back to the mansion of the party she'd crashed and would have tried to track me down.

Unless she wanted nothing to do with me.

It wasn't like we were anything more than a one-night stand.

I'm standing in the kitchen, barefoot. I have thrown on a pair of blue jeans and a black t-shirt. I'll shower and get dressed after breakfast.

Alessandro is out for the morning, which gives me an extra hour to make sure things are going smoothly with Karina and the boy, Ashton.

The soft patter of footsteps tromps through the open kitchen door.

The sunlight casts across him as he stands beside Karina. "Come, have a seat," she instructs, bringing him to the counter where there's a stool to sit.

"Ashton, I'd like you to meet Aurielo," Karina introduces us.

I wipe the flour from my hands on my pants. Not my best move. My blue jeans have a nice coating of white on them with handprints.

He scrunches his nose and smiles at my gesture. He's all grins and sunshine. This place will darken him.

I'll darken him.

Not that I want to, but everything I touch turns to darkness.

Happiness is fleeting.

I hold out my hand. "It's nice to meet you, Ashton."

Ashton stares at my hand. I don't know if he has an aversion to shaking hands or just doesn't know what to do.

I close my fist and offer a fist bump.

His eyes narrow, and he lifts his hand into a fist and bumps my knuckles with his.

Progress.

Baby steps. I'll take it.

Ashton is likely as stubborn as his mother.

Why do I bother trying? Because I take marriage seriously. Maybe this isn't how I imagined I'd meet my wife, marry, and start a family.

But I won't accept her in the arms of any other man.

She's mine.

Until death do us part.

Those are the vows we took, making her my wife. And I intend to honor them, commitment, and all.

"Do you like pancakes?" I ask Ashton.

Karina lifts him to sit on the stool at the counter, and she hovers behind him.

I can't tell if she's a helicopter parent or just keeping him close because she doesn't trust me. Not that I blame her.

It's not like we know each other. We're strangers, except that we had sex.

Once.

And everything I do to try to put her out of my mind, I find it damn near impossible. The woman practically glows, especially around Ashton.

Is that what real love is like?

"Can I have French Toast?" he quips.

I already have the mixing bowl out and started with the ingredients to make pancakes.

"Ashton," Karina scolds him. "You like pancakes."

"I like pancakes the way you make them," he says. "But Ivy made mushy pancakes for breakfast yesterday, and she made me eat them."

Ashton scrunches his nose in disgust. "Those aren't the box kind."

"No, they're not. I promise mine aren't mushy," I say. I'm a connoisseur around the kitchen.

"Fine," Ashton says.

The kid probably won't even try my pancakes, and hell, if they don't turn out perfectly, I'll never get in this kid's good graces.

Why do I even try?

I grab the mixing bowl and head to the trash can, hitting the foot pedal and opening the lid. I dump the half-mixed contents into the garbage.

"What are you doing?" Karina asks.

"Making the kid French Toast." I drop the contents of the dirty bowls into the sink and grab a loaf of bread from the bread box.

Karina glances from Ashton to me before opening the fridge and retrieving the carton of eggs.

"It's fine." I grab the cinnamon and sugar mixture from the pantry and butter from the fridge and start preparing the ingredients into a fresh bowl.

Karina comes up beside me, standing next to me as I prepare the mixture. "Thank you," she whispers.

"Don't mention it."

I'm not trying to be grumpy. It's not like I'm around kids, ever. My younger brother, Giovan, isn't married and doesn't have a family. Even Nico, who got married six years ago, still doesn't have kids.

It's not like being in the mafia is conducive to raising a kid and having a family.

We make a lot of enemies, and I don't want my family to find their lives put on the line. It's why I swore that I'd never marry.

Of course, I didn't expect to find myself ordered to kill *her*, either.

Maybe I should have gone through with it.

But the truth is she stirred a raw, primal feeling inside of me.

I've slept with dozens of women, but she's the only one I wanted to see again, probably because I didn't have her phone number or know where she lived.

And killing her seemed ruthless.

Knowing that she had a kid, I'm glad I didn't follow Alessandro's orders. I could never have forgiven myself for murdering a mother.

The men we slaughter are scumbags, thieves, and snitches.

I don't take pleasure in making men suffer or interrogating them.

It's my job.

And sure, I may be good at it, but it doesn't mean I'm passionate about destroying someone's life and putting a bullet in their head.

———

"Do you have a minute?" Giovan asks.

I'm perched at my desk in the office. "Yeah, come in." While an interrogator, I also do a bit of reconnaissance and helping nab dirty thieves, which gives me a desk and my own private office. It's small but sufficient.

Giovan shuts the office door behind himself.

I'm not sure who he's worried about overhearing whatever he wants to say. Karina and Ashton are already gone for the day. Francesco dropped Ashton off at school and then shuttled Karina to work downtown.

"I want to have a word with you," Giovan says.

"Sure, have at it." I gesture for him to sit across from me on the black leather sofa against the wall.

"I don't know how to put this delicately, but did you see Ashton?"

"Yes, I made breakfast for the kid. He insisted he wanted French Toast this morning, and then after I tossed out the pancake batter that I had made, he took two bites of his French Toast and insisted that he was full!"

I pinch the bridge of my nose.

Kids give me a headache.

Well, one kid anyway.

"Maybe it's just a coincidence, but the kid looks exactly like you did at his age." He scrambles a photo out of his palm that he'd been hiding and stands, putting it on my desk for me to stare at.

"The resemblance is uncanny," I remark.

How could I not notice?

Giovan folds his arms across his chest. "I knew you didn't offer to marry her out of the goodness of your heart. The kid is yours, isn't he? How long have you known?"

"What?" He has to be crazy. "He's not mine."

"You've never had sex with Karina?" Giovan asks.

The old photograph stares back at me. My mouth is dry. Sweat beads on my forehead. "Well, there was one time, but it was years ago."

"Five years ago?" Giovan asks.

"About six," I say.

"Well, given that it takes nine months to gestate."

"She isn't an alien." I snort at his remark and glance up at my younger brother. "Besides, if it were my kid, Karina would have told me."

Giovan raises an eyebrow.

I don't know how the hell he does that.

"When?" Giovan asks.

I throw my hands into the air. "How about when I discovered that she had a son?"

"If I had to bet, I'd put money on it that the boy is yours," Giovan says. "If it were me, I'd take a DNA sample. Get the kid to give you a mouth swab or hair sample. Whatever it takes and send it in to be tested. Quickly and quietly."

I can't imagine the kid being quiet about anything. Ashton seems like a momma's boy, but then again, it's not like his father is in the picture.

Why is that?

I don't want to believe that Ashton could be mine. I lift the picture from the desk, staring at the image of myself from when I was five.

The resemblance is striking.

He's mine.

I know he's my son. I feel it in the pit of my stomach. The ache of worry and dread that she hid her pregnancy from me. That she hid *him* from me.

What did Karina tell her son about his father? Did she lie to him, just like she lied to me?

# 18

## KARINA

After having Francesco drive us to Ashton's school, he escorts me to work, just like yesterday.

"Ivy is going to have to pick Ashton up at four o'clock. She doesn't know how to get to the house," I say.

"I'll handle pickup. You haven't been in contact with Ivy since yesterday," Francesco says.

He isn't wrong about speaking with Ivy, but there's no way the school will let Ashton leave with a stranger. "You're not on the approved list," I say.

"Approved what?" He glances at me like I'm speaking a foreign language.

"The teacher won't let Ashton leave with a stranger. It's for his protection. Kidnappings and whatnot." I don't point out the fact that Francesco is a scary-looking dude. No way would he even attempt to pass as anything but a mobster.

"Have your sister drop him off at the hospital after school." He hands me his phone.

"I can call her at work," I say. We're almost in the lobby.

He glances at me out of the corner of his eye. "Very well."

I leave him in the lobby while I head to the elevator and up to the pediatric unit.

"Good morning," Jocelyn says.

"Morning," I answer.

I'm late again. It's a habit I can't afford to continue. I'm expecting the dragon to breathe fire down my neck, but she's nowhere in sight.

I hurry down the hall to get into my work clothes, remove my jewelry and valuables, and place the contents in my locker.

Jocelyn follows me. "Husband keeping you up late?" she teases.

She has no idea what's going on in my life. I want to tell her, but I can't. It's complicated, and it could endanger her life, which I don't want to do.

"Something like that. Have you seen the boss?" I ask, careful not to call her the dragon if she's around the corner. That would be just my luck to have her surface.

"Yeah, she's in a chipper mood. Your new hubby had donuts and bagels brought in from the bakery around the corner. I'm in love with him already," Jocelyn says and swoons. "When can we meet him?"

"You can't." I nip that suggestion immediately.

Her face falls. "Why not?"

I shove my clothes into the locker and lace up my sneakers for my shift. "Because he's extremely private."

I want to confide in her, but at the same time, I'm afraid that this new sugary sweet Jocelyn that Aurielo has managed to create by buttering her up with sweets and breakfast treats will backfire on me.

"He dropped off the baked goods in person this morning and spoke with the dragon," Jocelyn says with a smirk.

"He did what?" My mouth drops at her remark. She can't be serious.

A huge grin spreads across her face. "I had you!"

"You're a brat," I retort and slam my locker shut. "I'm going to tell him to quit sending pastries because you don't deserve anything sweet."

"Fine, but the bagels look delicious too!"

I groan and roll my eyes as I head down the hallway in the opposite direction to check on my patients.

———

"Is it true you just got married?" Cora asks.

She's fourteen and one of my favorite patients. Cora has been in and out of the hospital since I started working there.

"Who told you?" I laugh. No one can keep a secret.

"Nurse Jocelyn was blabbing about the donuts this morning. Do you have a picture of him?"

"I don't," I say.

She gives me a confused look. "You don't have a picture of your husband. How about when he was your fiancé?" Cora is smart. A little too smart for her own good sometimes.

"Nope."

Her eyes narrow. "Not even on your phone?" Cora holds out her hand, expecting me just to hand over my device.

I love the kid, but she has no boundaries, just like Jocelyn.

"My phone is toast. I have a cheap replacement, but it's not a smartphone."

"Lame," she says.

I check her vitals and make notes on her chart for the doctor.

"Tell me what he's like. Let me live vicariously through you," Cora says. She sits up farther in bed.

I've never seen Cora quite so eager before. She's perked up, and her cheeks are a little more rosy than usual. I'd worry it's due to an infection and fever, but her temperature is normal.

"He's got lots of tattoos on his arms, tall, handsome, and has an accent."

"What kind of accent?"

"He's Italian," I say.

"Oh man, he must be hot!"

I scribble down a few more readings. "Scary is more like it," I mutter under my breath.

"What was that?" Cora asks.

Nothing gets by her. Ever.

"You have a kid, right?"

I nod slowly, not sure where she's going with this new line of questioning. "That's right, a boy." She's seen his photograph on my phone. He was my background picture practically since he was born.

"What's your new husband think of becoming a dad?"

I groan. The kid might be fourteen, but she's a world ahead in the way her mind works. Right now, I wish that I'd checked on Molly next door, who is six. She's sweet, a chatterbox, and doesn't ask me anything personal.

"He's still adjusting," I say.

"Ouch," Cora says and smirks.

It's like the kid can see right through me.

Maybe everyone can, and that's why they're asking me about Aurielo?

"What does the father think?" Cora asks.

"That's enough questions," I say, clearing my throat. "You should be resting."

Cora whines. "That's all I ever get to do. I want to hear all about your love life."

"Nice try."

————

Sitting at the nurses' station, sipping a bottle of water and typing up notes, I glance up when I feel someone staring at me.

"Aurielo?"

What the hell is he doing here?.

I save the file and quickly scamper around to grab him by the lapels and drag him into the breakroom.

"We need to talk," he says.

I shut the door behind us.

"You couldn't wait until I got home from work tonight to discuss whatever is on your mind?" I can't believe he has the nerve to just show up while I'm at work!

"Is it true?" He steps closer, cornering me in the small, enclosed room.

"Is what true?" I stare up into his dark, stern gaze. He's dressed to the nines in his suit coat. He looks every bit a businessman and out of place in the hospital.

Truthfully, I prefer the ensemble that I saw him in this morning, casual and sexy, but it's not like it matters.

We're married, but it's not out of love.

"That Ashton is my son." His hands are balled into fists at his side. He stares at me, waiting for me to answer him.

Is he expecting me to confirm his suspicions?

"Ashton isn't yours." There's no father marked on the birth certificate. It isn't like I knew how to reach him, not that I tried, either.

"Don't lie to me!" his voice bellows. My arms tingle, and I shiver. "Giovan suggested I take a DNA test and compare mine with Ashton's."

I lick my lips. "You don't want to do that."

"And why not?" he asks, leaning closer. He pulls something from his pocket, shoving it in my face.

I reach for the faded photograph, examining it thoroughly. The image looks so much like Ashton.

"That's me," Aurielo says, clarifying his point. "I look just like Ashton at that age."

I open my mouth and glance past Aurielo for the door. It's shut. The window is frosted. No one is likely to come in and check on us anytime soon.

"A lot of kids have similar features," I whisper.

"Are you really going to lie to my face, *Micetta*?"

My bottom lip trembles. I don't want to be afraid, but I worry about my son. His safety and the man he'll become if he looks up to Aurielo.

"You're a monster," I whisper, staring up into his darkened irises. "I don't want my son to become like you."

"This monster saved your life. Don't you ever forget that, *Micetta,*" Aurielo says and turns, storming out of the breakroom.

# 19

## AURIELO

I didn't plan on going to the hospital to have a word with Karina. But after Giovan suggested what I already feared, I had to see her. It couldn't wait until tonight.

It would be easy to sneak a DNA test, hide it from Karina and find out the truth.

But I'm not a man to do things behind someone's back.

If Ashton is mine, she owes me the truth.

If he's not, then I want to know who the father is and why he isn't in their lives.

What type of man abandons his son?

My questions quickly turn to an interrogation. My methods aren't cruel or unkind, and I refrain from trapping her against the wall physically, but my eyes pin her.

She's shivering as she speaks, her body betraying her.

"Are you really going to lie to my face, *Micetta*?"

Her bottom lip trembles as she speaks, her voice barely above a whisper. "You're a monster. I don't want my son to become like you."

How can she forget what I did for her?

"This monster saved your life. Don't you ever forget that, *Micetta*."

I can't stand to be around her. I storm out of the breakroom and down the hallway. I'm trying to be quiet and not bring more attention to myself, but it's impossible as my footfalls pound the floor.

She lied to me.

Karina had every opportunity to deny my questions, claim I'm crazy and that Ashton isn't my child.

But that isn't what happened.

I want to be wrong. And at the same time, knowing that the boy who will be coming home tonight after school is my child, it burns right through my very existence.

My legs burn, my feet are like fire against the ground. I want to run.

But my suit is suffocating.

I hurry down the hallway and hit the button for the elevator repeatedly. Not that it hurries the car any quicker, but it makes me feel better, like I'm doing something instead of standing around.

I step into the elevator and turn around.

Karina is staring back at me from across the open expanse of the hallway. Her eyes look distraught. Her bottom lip is curled like she's trying not to cry.

I can't comfort her.

Not now.

Maybe not ever.

She's not mine.

Inside the elevator, I feel trapped. I'm relieved when the bell dings and the doors open. I hurry out and down to the lobby, catching sight of Francesco.

"Everything okay?" he asks.

"Just peachy," I mutter. "Walk with me." I head outside, and he follows my orders.

Since there's no current threat to Karina, she doesn't need Francesco in the hospital lobby. He's here on Alessandro's orders to make sure that she doesn't flee. If the girl wanted to run, she would.

She still might.

And knowing the boy could be mine, I can't let her leave.

One problem at a time, though. Convincing her that she wants to stay is the priority.

"What do you know about private schools?" I ask.

Francesco gives me a funny look. "What's this about?"

Could he be that stupid to ask? "Ashton."

What other kid is there around the house?

"I'd recommend looking into boarding schools," Francesco says.

It's certainly crossed my mind, but I'm not sure I'm ready to send the kid away if he's mine. I want to get to know Ashton, not send him to some prestigious educational facility, only to see him during holidays and summer vacation.

Plus, I doubt Karina would be onboard with sending the boy away, either.

"He's five. Let's save that suggestion for his teenage years when things are even more complicated," I mutter.

He shoves his hands into his pockets. "I don't know of any private schools specifically, but I can do a little research on my phone while I'm waiting for your wife."

It sounds strange to hear Francesco refer to Karina as my wife, but he isn't wrong.

"Don't worry about it." I can do the same when I get back to the compound. "I just thought if you heard anything good or bad about any of the private schools locally, I'd ask first."

"I'm just glad you're thinking about putting him in a school up north. We dropped him off this morning for school, and her twin sister is picking him up and bringing him to the hospital lobby after school."

"Ivy's bringing Ashton to the hospital?" I stop walking as we reach the end of the block, and it's either cross the street or turn around.

I turn around, and Francesco follows. My stomach is somersaulting. I don't trust Ivy, and I don't want her around my kid.

"Why aren't you picking him up?"

"Karina mentioned that the school won't let him leave without it being an approved guardian or parent."

"Fuck," I mutter under my breath. "Do you have the address?"

He retrieves his cell phone and texts me the information. "Not sure what good it will do. Karina was adamant that I couldn't pick the kid up. Ivy had to do it."

"We'll see about that."

———

After leaving the hospital, I head to the nearest store to pick up a booster seat for the vehicle. Traffic is a mess, and the lady at the checkout counter takes twice as long as necessary.

I glance at my watch as I pull up outside the elementary school. Cars are lined up around the block.

Quickly, I park and hustle down the sidewalk. The kids haven't been let out yet.

"What are you doing here?" Ivy asks, catching sight of me. She folds her arms across her chest and gives me a disapproving stare.

"Picking up Ashton," I say.

Why else would I be hanging around an elementary school? It's not like I have dozens of kids running around the city.

At least I don't think I do, but I've slept with my fair share of women.

"Checking up on me? Worried I wouldn't bring him to Karina's work."

She's not entirely wrong, but I know Karina trusts her sister, and that's enough for me. "It's none of your business why I'm here."

I'm not sure why I'm even here. There is a shit ton of work to get done, and if Alessandro gets wind that I'm playing house instead of following up a lead for him, I'll have to face his wrath, which isn't fun.

But I also want to get to know the kid.

My kid.

Karina may as well have confirmed that to me this morning. She had every opportunity to tell me that the kid isn't mine. That I'm crazy for thinking he is my kin.

No.

Instead, she pointed out that I'm a monster, and she doesn't want Ashton to become like me.

I intend to prove to her that I'm not the beast she believes me to be. I'm just not sure how that's going to happen.

"You're wasting your time," Ivy says.

I take the bait. "Why's that?"

"Do you want to be stuck in the car with a five-year-old asking a million questions on the drive home?" Ivy smirks. "You probably don't know anything about kids, let alone how to deal with them."

Why am I arguing with Karina's sister? The woman tried to trick me into believing that she was Karina!

My hands bunch into fists at my sides. "You will let me take Ashton home with me."

"Or what?" Ivy drops her hands to her sides. "You'll fight me? You're easily twice my size, but I can outrun you."

That woman has a mouth on her.

"You would think that," I say and lean closer, "but I ran track and field in high school."

"What was that, a century ago?" Ivy quips.

Although I have a few years on Ivy and Karina, I'm not that much older. She's just trying to get under my skin, and she's doing a hell of a job at it.

She's infuriating to be around. It's incredible how they're twins and nothing alike. The similarities end with their appearance.

Sure, Karina has a mouth on her, but it's a pair of lips that I want to devour. With Ivy, all I feel is the sting of anger at her betrayal, pushing Karina to the floor. Maybe it was an act of selflessness, but all I see is the bitch standing in front of me.

The doors to the school open and the kids pour out in a mess of chaos. Ashton rushes toward Ivy.

"You came!" Ashton grins. "I missed you this morning."

"I'll bet you missed my pancakes," Ivy says.

I snort at her remark.

Ashton's eyes widen with a huge grin, and he glances at me wondering if I'll keep his secret.

Don't worry, kid. I don't need to get on your bad side. I already have your mother and aunt to deal with, which is more than enough trouble.

Ivy has to sign out for Ashton, which takes a few minutes for the teacher to come around with the clipboard.

"I'm Aurielo, Karina's husband," I say, shaking hands and introducing myself to Ashton's teacher.

She's short, barely five feet, and wearing a long, flowing dress that matches her deep brunette hair.

"Oh, I didn't realize she was married! I'm Ms. Brown," the woman says.

I bite my tongue. That won't be hard to remember.

"We recently tied the knot," I say, giving a warm smile and firm handshake.

We exchange brief pleasantries before she rushes off to the next parent.

"Why *did* you marry my sister?" Ivy asks, emphasizing her question. She grabs Ashton's hand and heads away from the school, down the sidewalk.

"I parked that way." I point in the opposite direction that we're heading. I can see my car parked on the street.

"Do you have a car seat?" She stops in front of her mini crunch car.

"Yes, I bought one on the way here," I smirk, pleased that I have one-upped her.

"Well, I'm not relinquishing him to you. My sister told me to bring him over to her work."

She pops the trunk of the car.

"What are you doing?" She's not going to put the kid in the trunk, is she?

The car is a two-door, barely any space, and if anyone hits the back of the vehicle, they'll crush the life out of my son.

"This is your car?" I ask.

She takes Ashton's backpack and drops it tersely into the trunk, slamming the lid shut.

"Yeah. So?"

"My son isn't riding in the backseat of that deathtrap!"

She has to be crazy thinking it's safe to drive him around the city in that two-door piece of crap.

"He's ridden in it every day after school until you decided to show up and be a father to your son!"

"Excuse me?"

"You heard me!" Ivy snarls at me and steps closer, jabbing my chest with her finger. "You deserted my sister after you knocked her up! What kind of person does that? She told you she was pregnant, and you said you wanted nothing to do with her."

"Whoa!" I knock her arms down and take a step back. "Karina never came to me. She didn't tell me a damned thing about being pregnant. I married her to protect her and save her life. I had no clue she was a mother, let alone the kid was mine."

Her face turns ghastly. Her eyes are wide in horror.

Is she going to be sick?

"She told me she reached out to the father."

"Well, it wasn't me."

Am I not the kid's father? Does Ashton have a father out there who abandoned him? Or did Karina lie to her sister?

She rubs at her temples. "I can't have this conversation with you. I don't even like you."

"Feeling's mutual," I retort. Not that there's a rule against having conversations with people I don't like. I have plenty of them, usually in dark cellars or the basement prison.

## 20

### KARINA

I glance at my watch. The day seems to drag on forever, but by the time I get off and head downstairs, Ashton should be arriving with Ivy.

There's no way I could make it by three o'clock to pick him up.

Ivy is a lifesaver.

She's also a bit of a spitfire and a healthy dose of trouble, but I love my sister.

I change out of my work clothes and head for the elevator with Jocelyn. "I still want to hear everything about your new hubby," she says. "How you met, what he's like in bed. Give me the details, girl! I caught a glimpse of him, and he's swoon-worthy."

"What does that even mean?" I ask.

"Tall, dark, handsome. Oh, and the tattoos are even sexier. I'll bet he makes your panties melt," Jocelyn says with a wicked grin.

"Shut it!" I warn her as we step into the elevator.

She smirks. "You should be coming into work glowing after your wedding night. Girl, you need a honeymoon!"

I roll my eyes.

"Not easy with a kid, a full-time job, you know, life."

Not to mention the basic fact we're not in love.

What I need is for her to stop talking about Aurielo. But I doubt she will, and the fact we're going to run into Francesco isn't going to help matters. She'll have more questions.

We ride down the elevator, and I'm relieved when the bell dings and we reach the ground floor for the lobby.

Together, we step out, and she follows beside me as I head toward the waiting area.

I bite down on my bottom lip. Why is Aurielo here? And Ivy hasn't left, either. She doesn't look the least bit happy.

Aurielo is the last person I want to deal with, especially right now with Jocelyn at my side. She has no idea who he is or why we married. And I can't tell her. I don't want to endanger her life.

But I'm confident someone will spill the truth.

"Hi!" Jocelyn squeals and offers out her hand to Aurielo. "Family reunion?" she jokes, noticing my sister.

"Something like that," he says and gives me a confused glance.

"Sorry," I say, quick to apologize. "Aurielo, this is my coworker, Jocelyn."

"Coworker?" Jocelyn scoffs. "We're besties. I was in the delivery room with Karina. That makes me family."

"Only because I faint at the sight of blood," Ivy says. "And I didn't want to see this guy coming out." She ruffles Ashton's hair.

He scrunches his face. "Gross!"

"It's nice to meet you," Aurielo says, shaking Jocelyn's hand as they exchange pleasantries.

I grab Ivy by the arm, pulling her close. "What's going on?" I expect an honest answer from my sister. I didn't anticipate that she'd hang around when dropping Ashton off, but they probably just arrived.

Although it doesn't explain what Aurielo is doing here too.

"Aurielo showed up at pickup today," Ivy fumes. "He insulted my car, and he insisted that you never told him about the kid." She keeps her voice down, which I appreciate. It's not a conversation I want everyone to hear.

"Well, I didn't."

"What?" she squeals. "You told me that he told you to take care of it, and he wanted nothing to do with you."

I grimace. "I said that?" I never thought my little white lie would slap me in the face.

"Yeah, pretty sure you did," Ivy says. "Anyway, he knows he's the father."

Great. I exhale a sharp sigh. "Come on, kiddo. Let's get you home." I pull Ashton in for a squeeze hug. It's a ritual I enjoy partaking in every time I get off work and see my boy.

He has no idea how lucky he is to be healthy. The kids I see on the unit and what they endure break my heart nearly every day.

"Mom, you're squeezing me to death," Ashton groans.

Gosh, he sounds like a teenager already.

Jocelyn says goodbye and heads out the main door. Ivy joins her, heading out to the parking garage.

"How about the three of us take a drive together," Aurielo suggests.

I glance at Francesco.

Is that allowed?

"If you don't require my services, I'll return to the complex," Francesco says.

Aurielo and Francesco exchange a few words in Italian that I don't understand. Maybe I'll start taking Italian lessons in secret. That way, I'll know what they're saying if they're talking about me.

Although that's a lot of work and requires time. Something I don't have a lot of between work and a kid.

I reach for Ashton's backpack seated on the lobby chair. It's light, but he's also in kindergarten. He's brought a few assignments and homework home, but never textbooks.

"Come on," Aurielo says, gesturing for us to follow him outside. "Let me carry that," he offers, holding out his hand.

I hand over the bag, and I take Ashton's hand as Aurielo walks beside me. Every so often, he glances at Ashton.

"Are we still fighting?" Aurielo asks.

"You tell me." I glance at him. He knows how I feel. I made it clear earlier. I don't want my son to grow up to become a monster.

It scares me what he'll see and experience inside the house where we now live.

The exterior is beautiful, a mansion, but behind the beautiful four walls, there are more sinister dealings and business transactions.

I just hope Aurielo doesn't do his interrogations at the house.

The other day he'd been at a hotel torturing a gentleman who had been tied up. That seemed like a terrible place to do business. Don't they worry about housekeeping stumbling into their room?

Is that how they manage to get their dangerous mafia men married?

No.

I'm an exception.

Aurielo suggested that we marry. He was trying to protect me.

"I don't want to fight with you, but we have a lot to discuss. In private."

He escorts me out to his vehicle, and I glance in the backseat, relieved that he's already thought this through. There's a booster seat for Ashton.

Ashton climbs into the backseat, and once I'm confident that he's buckled and secure, I climb into the front seat of the SUV.

It's roomy and smells like new leather.

Aurielo climbs into the driver's seat and starts the engine.

"Where are we going?" I ask.

"For a drive," Aurielo says.

Cryptic.

"You don't plan on offing us. Do you? Tell me now, and we'll get out of your hair, disappear. You never have to see us again."

His eyes narrow as he shoots a glance at me. "Is that a joke?" He doesn't sound the least bit amused.

It wasn't a joke, but I'm not sure I want to give all my secrets away. I swallow nervously and force a smile. "Not funny?"

"No, I don't find it humorous to suggest my wife run away with my son."

"That's a conversation for later," I say, keeping my voice down so that only Aurielo can hear me.

We pull out of the parking garage and navigate through the city. I glance back at Ashton and give him a warm, reassuring smile.

I don't think Aurielo will kill us or hurt us. But the truth is I have to keep my guard up because how can I trust a man I barely know? I may have thrown myself into danger by marrying him, but I have to look out for Ash.

"Are we heading back?" We're traveling north, with the lakefront to our east, but he's silent.

"No. I told you, I'm taking you somewhere—special," he says.

I press my lips together. I can't fathom where he's taking us. The museums downtown are in the opposite direction.

"Any hints?"

His hands are clenched on the steering wheel, his grip fierce.

"You're not a spontaneous person. Are you?" he asks.

He isn't wrong. It wasn't my idea to crash the party that night with my sister. Not that I have any regrets,

I honestly don't. If I hadn't gone along with her crazy plan, I'd have never had Ashton.

"Is it that obvious?" I mutter.

"Relax," Aurielo says. "I wouldn't take my son anywhere dangerous."

## 21

## AURIELO

Karina has no idea where we're going, not that I expect her to guess correctly. I've given her no indication and no hints.

She's squirming in the front seat, her fingers rubbing over her legs.

One glance, and I can feel her nervous energy seeping out of her.

"Mommy, I'm hungry," Ashton whines from the backseat.

Shit.

I don't have any snacks. I can take them both out to eat after I reveal the surprise.

I am assuming the kid won't melt down and throw a fit from hunger first.

She digs into her purse and retrieves a plastic baggy with peanut butter crackers inside. It's any miracle they're not squished.

"Here you go," she says, handing it to him in the backseat.

"Try not to leave crumbs," I mutter. The car is still pristine and smells like a new car. It has less than ten thousand miles on the odometer.

"Oops," Ashton says between bites of his snack, the rustling of plastic against his fingers.

"I will vacuum your car and clean out the mess," Karina says. "Please don't be mad at him."

I glance up in the rearview mirror, and Ashton's grin is wide, his face messy with cracker crumbs, but it doesn't bother him. He's so carefree and innocent.

I don't ever remember life being that simple, not even when I was a child.

I pull off the main road and take a side street toward the intended destination. We've been driving for a while, the city is no longer in the rearview mirror.

"Are we almost there?" Karina asks.

"Yes," I say, not giving anything further away. My gaze slips from the road to her as she's seated beside me.

Her hands are wrung together, and her tongue darts out and swipes her lips. I want to lean across the seat and press my mouth against hers, taste her, touch her, devour her.

But I can't do that.

I won't do that.

She's a fantasy that I can't indulge in.

At least I shouldn't.

Karina is too sweet, too pure, too innocent.

I'll destroy her, even without meaning to.

I refocus my attention back to the road, pull up to the one-story cottage, and park the vehicle.

"We're here." I open the door and step out, stretching my legs.

She climbs out of the car before opening the back door, letting Ashton out while I stalk up the porch steps.

The house is rustic and old. There are cobwebs on the porch, and I swat them away, digging out my key to unlock the front door.

"This is your place?" Karina hesitates.

"No, I'm house-sitting."

She frowns, not gathering it's a joke.

The plot of land stretches onto open fields with no neighbors nearby. The land is wild, and it feels like another world just outside of the city. We've actually crossed state lines but it's not that far from the compound.

"Relax," I say. "The place is mine. My grandfather passed his property on to me when he died."

"Oh, why don't you live here if you own the house?"

She follows me inside as I hit the lights. The electricity still works. I pay the bills on the property since it's in my name.

I never needed to sell the place. The thought of parting with it was too painful. There were lots of good memories, spending summers with my grandfather up here. And there's always the opportunity to get away from the world by coming here.

I also have a bachelor pad in the city where I used to take the ladies for a wild night.

Another secret she doesn't need the details to.

"Alessandro has been generous in letting me stay with him. It's allowed me to climb the ranks quite fast, being under his scrutiny."

Her brow tightens as she gazes over the furniture and takes in the surroundings.

"I know it's not much."

She wanders toward an end table with photographs, lifting one of the frames and studying the picture.

I come up behind her, glancing over her shoulder at the photo of my grandpa and me camping. The little boy in the picture looks so much like Ashton. The resemblance is uncanny.

"It's perfect," she whispers, placing the frame carefully back onto the table. "Why take us here?"

"Do you want to play catch?" I ask Ashton, heading toward the bedroom closet.

My old room from when I'd visit as a kid.

Ashton is silent as I head down the hallway.

Even though I only came for summers, Grandpa insisted that the room would always be mine. I had a home with him, no matter what.

I open the closet, and on the top shelf is a baseball and glove, just as I'd left it.

"You've played catch before, right?" I ask, ushering him out through the front door and around to the side of the house, away from the vehicle.

Ashton hesitates, and Karina follows, her hands on his shoulders.

"Go play. You'll have fun."

He putters behind. I hand him the baseball, showing him the proper way to hold the ball and follow through with his throw.

Keeping the mitt for myself, I take a few steps back, letting him toss the ball.

His aim is way off, but he's got a strong arm, and I have to make sure he doesn't hit a window on the first couple of throws.

But after a few minutes, he quickly gets the hang of throwing the ball at me.

I want to be the kind of father for Ashton that I never had.

Karina leans against the house, arms folded. "You mind if I take a walk?" she asks.

"Go ahead. When you come back, we can go out to dinner."

She pushes herself off the side of the house and heads around the house. I'm not sure where she's going, but the neighborhood is safe. The same can't be said for where her apartment is located.

"Are you having fun?" I ask Ashton.

His eyes tighten before he throws me a fast pitch. It has a little bite and isn't nearly as wild as the last throw.

He's a quick study.

"Can I get a baseball bat?" he asks. "I've always wanted to play like they do on television!"

It's amazing how the kid can brighten my day. Chuckling, I toss the ball lightly back to him to catch before he throws another sharp pitch right into my glove.

Alessandro will have a fit if one of the balls hits the mansion, let alone busts a window.

But how can I tell the kid no?

"You sure can. Now I know what to get you for your birthday."

Ashton whines. "My birthday is forever away. It'll be winter and cold."

"I'll bet there's a baseball bat somewhere around the house that we can find."

"Here?" Ashton asks and drops the ball at his feet, glancing back at the cottage.

I meant the mansion where we live, but that bat would probably have blood and other excrements from being used as a weapon. "No. How about you give me one last good throw, and then we find your mom?"

Ashton bends down and lifts the baseball from the ground. He throws me the ball, this time with a spin and a curve.

He giggles and laughs as I leap to catch the ball, nearly missing it.

The roar of an engine brings me rushing toward Ashton and lifting him in my arms, over my shoulder as the impending vehicle approaches the cottage.

He's laughing, oblivious to my concern.

"What are you doing?" he squeals.

Slowly, I put him down, keeping him hidden behind me against the side of the house. "Shh," I warn him, a finger against my lips.

"We have to be quiet."

# 22

## KARINA

The house is small and quaint. Not anything I'd expect from a man living in a mansion and working for the mafia.

Why show me the house?

Why take me here?

Is he trying to show me what it was like growing up, being with his grandfather?

I can't wrap my head around it, but the peacefulness is too surreal. I haven't heard anything more than the wind and birds as I walk along the gravel road dividing the field.

There's no sign of civilization.

No other houses nearby, but we passed a few before turning onto the road. I assume it's a private street.

His grandfather owned quite a bit of land.

Was he in the mafia too?

How did Aurielo end up working as an interrogator?

Whatever the reason, I'm not sure I want to know his story or will like hearing it.

In the distance, the roar of an engine startles me. It's coming from the opposite direction of the house.

I step off the road, and the SUV rushes by, kicking up dust and dirt as it barrels down the road for the cottage.

Two more identical SUVs follow.

My stomach flops, and the hairs on my arms stand on end.

Something is wrong.

I can feel it deep inside of me.

Ashton is in danger.

I tear down the road, tripping over my feet when I near the cottage. All three black SUVs, the same ones that I witnessed barreling down the road minutes earlier, are parked out front, blocking Aurielo's vehicle.

I retrieve my burner cell phone from my pocket.

There's no reception.

Who would I even call? I don't have Francesco's phone number, and my sister can't help. Do I try the cops?

I don't have a weapon or anything useful to use in defending myself or my son.

I sneak around the back of one of the empty SUVs and peek through the window, trying to see what's happening, and glance inside for any spare guns or tools.

There's a black bag in the trunk, but I don't wait around to open it and find out what's buried inside.

I hurry from one SUV to the next, getting a closer look at the scene in front of me.

Six men have their guns poised at Aurielo. It's a bit of overkill for one man.

He pissed off someone.

I don't see Ashton.

Aurielo has his hands in the air. I don't see the ball or glove, not that I expect to, either.

"It's just me here, boys. You really are trying to overcompensate for something. I'd guess it's the size of your dicks."

I grimace at his words. It's not the kind of language that I want Ashton to overhear, but I'm relieved he's not turning the kid over to them, either.

"We heard you married some whore. Where is she?" Two of the men storm inside the house.

Several loud thuds and glass shatters as they break and tear apart his home. "We'll find her!"

I want to help, but I don't know how. Around the opposite side of the house, Ashton appears, his eyes wide, filled with tears.

I must get to him, protect him. Exhaling a sharp breath, I dart from behind one SUV to the next before making a quick beeline for the opposite side of the house from where the men are pointing their weapons at Aurielo.

"Did you see that?" one of the gunmen shouts.

Shit.

"Probably a coyote," Aurielo says casually.

I grab Ashton. His eyes are wide and glistening with tears. He's holding back his cries for help, and I'm grateful for the silence.

If he were smaller, I'd pick him up and run, but he's too big for me to carry without it slowing us down. I clutch his hand and drag him to follow me around to the back side of the house.

We keep low around the windows. There are men inside the cottage tearing the place apart, piece by piece.

Are they looking for something or someone?

What do they want?

Wouldn't they have killed Aurielo if they wanted him dead?

## 23

## AURIELO

"Run. Hide!" I shoot orders at Ashton.

He stares at me blankly.

The kid has no idea the danger that he's in, and Karina is nowhere in sight.

I can defend myself, but the kid, my son, I'll never forgive myself if anything happens to him. And without a doubt, I know Karina will hate me.

"Hide around back. Look for your mom, but you must be quiet. These are scary men." I hope it's enough of a warning for him to take shelter.

The first SUV is in sight, and behind it, two more barrel down the road to the cottage.

Dorian's men.

They have to be. Who else would come all this way to track me down?

There must have been surveillance on the cottage.

It's no secret my grandfather, the head of the Rinaldi family, owned the cottage and that it was passed on to me.

Why are they here?

What do they want?

Is this revenge because I ended things with Etta Bianchi?

The black SUV pulls up to an abrupt halt, slamming on the brakes.

Dorian steps out. He's tall, with thinning hair, and old enough to be my father.

His belly protrudes past his belt, the jacket unbuttoned because it's probably too tight to fit.

"Well, well, well. Look who we have here," Dorian says.

I press my lips tight. The longer I stall, the more time for Karina to return and find Ashton.

Where the hell is she?

Didn't she notice the three SUVs racing toward the cottage?

The doors slam as his minions pile out from the adjacent vehicles.

Six men in total.

I could take them, but not without risking Ashton and Karina.

Did Ashton listen to me? Is he hiding?

I can't chance glancing back over my shoulder. I don't want anyone to suspect that I'm here with anyone else.

If the property were under surveillance, then they'd know that I brought my family with me.

Family.

The words burn inside of me, ripping me apart.

This is why I swore I'd never get married. The job is too dangerous. I make too many enemies in my line of work.

And marrying Etta for a cease-fire between our families would never have lasted.

Etta and I weren't in love.

Dorian brandishes his gun, pointing it straight at my head. "Hands up!" he shouts.

He's overzealous. He probably hasn't had a kill in days, maybe even weeks. At least not as rich as me.

And I'm not talking about money. Not literally anyhow. Although I'm sure my head is worth top dollar to him, he wants his revenge because I broke his baby girl's heart.

At least, I assume that's why he's here.

Otherwise, he'd be attacking the compound if it's about power and money.

I throw my hands into the air. "Don't shoot." I step away from the house to keep Dorian or his men from noticing the baseball or glove buried against the side of the house.

"Where is she?"

Are they looking for Karina?

Why?

What does she have to do with Dorian and his crew?

"It's just me here, boys. You really are trying to overcompensate for something. I'd guess it's the size of your dicks," I say, trying to distract them.

I catch a brief glimpse of Karina. At least, I think it's her. There's a figure behind the SUV. It's too tall to be Ashton, and the build is a woman. Etta wouldn't accompany her father on his dirty business dealings.

"We heard you married some whore. Where is she?" Dorian asks.

When I don't answer, he gestures two of his men to the cottage. "Search the house. Tear it apart if you have to."

Two of his thugs stomp inside, destroying precious memories of my past. They're looking for Karina. They want her dead.

Glass shatters against the walls and floors.

They're tearing apart the house, destroying everything inside that belongs to me.

Where the hell do they think she's hiding?

Karina darts from the SUV to the opposite side of the house.

"You boys are barking up the wrong tree," I say, trying to distract them.

"Did you see that?" Dorian shouts.

Shit.

"Probably a coyote," I say with a shrug. "We get them all the time."

Dorian and his second in command rush to the opposite side after Karina.

I can easily take two men at once. Six without a weapon is more of a challenge.

I have to move quickly before Dorian and his second find Karina and Ashton. I jut my leg out, sweeping the shorter and stockier of the two men to the ground.

Using my palm, I slam my hand upward into the other man's nose and knee him in the groin, grabbing his gun as he doubles over.

"You fucking asshole!" He falls to the ground, clutching his family jewels while blood pours out his nose.

The first man rolls in the dirt, reaching for his gun, and I kick it farther out of his reach before snatching it from the ground, my newly acquired gun poised on his head.

"Don't move," I warn them both. "Or I'll put a bullet in both of your heads."

I rush around the opposite side of the house to chase after Dorian. I can't focus on the two men tearing apart the inside of what was once my grandfather's home.

Karina and Ashton are my priority.

I'm quiet and stealthy. It's any wonder that the two thugs I disarmed don't give me up. Are they as loyal to Dorian as he believes them to be?

Stalking up behind Dorian, I poise the gun against the back of his head. "Drop your weapon," I command.

A dark cackle spills from his lips. "Well played, Aurielo."

Ashton clutches Karina, but she shoves him behind her to protect her son.

"Leave us alone," Karina's voice doesn't quiver as she stares down Dorian.

The girl has no fear.

Or at least she hides it well.

"Did he tell you he's engaged to my daughter?" Dorian asks as he slowly lowers his gun and slides it back into its holster at his hip.

Karina doesn't flinch.

"I'm sorry to disappoint you, but whatever arrangement you previously had is null and void. I'm Aurielo Rinaldi's wife."

A grin spreads across my face, proud that Karina stands up to the bastard who tried to force me to marry his daughter.

Dorian turns around to face me. His second slowly lowers his weapon as well, but he doesn't return it to its holster.

"Congratulations on your marriage," Dorian says. His nostrils flare as he speaks. There's no humor or warmth in his remark, only fire behind his darkened gaze. "Just remember, it's till death do us part, and I'd say, my little girl, Etta, doesn't have much to worry about."

Dorian stalks past me, knocking into my shoulder as he heads for his vehicle. "Let's go!" he shouts to his men for them to follow.

I want to run over and check on Karina, but I keep two hands on my gun, the safety off, prepared for a firefight.

Dorian and his men gather in their vehicles, leaving as quickly as they came.

That was too easy. If Dorian wanted my bride and son dead, he could have easily pulled the trigger.

He was delivering a message. He's pissed that I didn't follow through and marry his daughter.

A warning.

You don't fuck with the Bianchis.

## 24

### KARINA

Dorian and his men drive off as quickly as they arrive.

"What the hell was that?" I shout at Aurielo.

I lift Ashton into my arms, wanting to shield him from danger, but it's already too late.

He's physically shaking in my arms. I rub his back and feel his wet face buried in my neck.

Aurielo shoves the gun into the waistband of his pants like it's just another typical day. Is this what I have to look forward to, married to him?

Ignoring me, he storms inside the house.

I stand outside, Ashton clinging to me.

The house is probably trashed. I could hear the men tearing apart his home, ransacking the place, but I'm unsure what they were after. Does he know?

Why won't he tell me what's going on?

"Are you going to answer me?" I shout at the open door.

Aurielo is inside the house, sifting through the destruction brought down by those men.

I step toward the house, climbing the three stairs up the porch, standing at the entrance to get a better look inside. Ashton is wrapped tight around my waist with his body, his arms snug around my neck.

I'm not stepping foot inside. There's broken glass on the floor, smashed pictures and furniture that's been ripped apart by knives, the stuffing spilled out.

"What were they looking for?" I ask, my voice calmer. Not that I feel an ounce of restraint, but I'm trying to understand what the hell just happened.

"I don't know," Aurielo says.

I'm not sure whether to believe him or not.

He grabs a few items spilled on the floor and picks them up, shoving them into a torn duffel bag. I'm not sure whether they damaged the bag, or it was old and worn.

I'd offer to help, but I have Ashton in my arms.

"Go wait in the car. I'll be done in a second," he says.

I press my lips tight, rolling them together, and concede. If Aurielo wants to be left alone, that's fine with me.

Heading to the SUV, I buckle Ashton into his booster seat.

"How are you doing?" I ask, the car door open as I give him my undivided attention.

At least he'll be honest with me. One of the advantages about kids, they don't sugarcoat shit.

"Who were those men?" Ashton asks.

"I don't know," I say. It's the truth. I could surmise that they're mafia, but what good does explaining that to him do? I don't want to scare him further. He'll probably have nightmares after today.

I'm sure I will.

"Are they coming back?" Ashton asks.

"If they do, we won't be here," I say and lean in, pressing a kiss to his cheek. I don't think they'll return today, and I'm confident we're leaving as soon as Aurielo is done gathering whatever mementos he wants from the house.

Aurielo hurries out of the house, slams the bullet-ridden door, and hustles down the steps. "Let's go," he says.

I shut the back door of the vehicle and stroll around the SUV to the passenger side. Aurielo pops the trunk and drops his duffel inside before jumping into the driver's seat and starting the engine.

"Change of plans," he says.

I glance at him, unsure what the original plans even were, but coming here was a mistake. I yank the seatbelt and snap the buckle in place while he puts the SUV into reverse and hurries us away from the house.

"We're heading straight back to the compound," Aurielo says. His focus is on the road, two hands gripping the steering wheel.

"Compound?"

"The house," he clarifies for me.

"Okay." I don't even remember if he said what he planned earlier for us. My stomach is still somersaulting, but my hands have finally stopped shaking.

"I'll make you both something to eat at the house."

Oh, right. Dinner.

How easy it is to forget everything else. The events of today feel like a lifetime away. I glance behind me at Ashton.

He's staring out the side window, silent.

It's probably for the best.

I reach for the radio, turning on the music.

Aurielo casts a glance at me. Like he's wondering what I'm doing, but he doesn't say a word.

It's been a long day.

I want to talk, but I don't want Ashton overhearing the conversation. "Can we talk about what just happened?" I ask, keeping my voice low.

"Now?" Aurielo glances in the rearview mirror. "Are you sure that's a good idea?"

"Just keep your voice down," I say. "Who is Etta Bianchi?" I recognize the name. It's the same one I used when I snuck into that party years ago. He'd told me she'd been his ex-girlfriend. But why had her name been on the invitation?

"My ex is the niece of Don Bianchi. Her parents died when she was a teenager, so he's raised her as his daughter."

"Were you two engaged?" I ask. I'm not sure I want to know the answer, but the fact they're exes at least tells me that I didn't break up an engagement.

"I never asked her to marry me or gave her a ring," Aurielo says.

We head off the side road and back onto the highway. Aurielo turns up the music, ending our conversation.

He's done talking.

I don't want to be done, but I'm not in the mood for a heated argument, either.

I fold my arms across my chest and glance out the side window. Dealing with kids who are dying is easier than talking with Aurielo.

I didn't expect to learn everything about him overnight when we married, but I thought his secrets and skeletons would stay locked up in the closet.

I certainly never expected they'd hunt us down, chase us with guns, and want to murder us.

However, they seemed more interested in threatening my son and me than Aurielo.

Why?

Is it because of Etta Bianchi?

Do they want us dead so he can marry her?

Although Ashton wouldn't have to die for that to happen.

Just me.

My mouth is parched, and I exhale a heavy sigh. The remainder of the ride is basked in silence. Aurielo doesn't attempt to converse. His knuckles are white on the steering wheel.

He's stressed, and based on the speed he's doing on the highway, he's also in a rush to get us back to the house.

He doesn't have to tell me he's worried. I can see the fear written all over his face.

I'm just not sure why.

We just met. He wouldn't be that upset if I died. It's not like he's in love with me. We hardly know each other.

Aurielo pulls through the open gate, and it quickly closes behind us. In a matter of minutes, we're ushered inside the house, and he tosses his keys at his brother.

"Can you park the car, Giovan?" he asks. "I've got a bag of Gramps' stuff in the trunk."

"You want me to unload the trunk too?" Giovan asks. The smirk falls from his face. "You look like shit. What the hell happened out there?"

Ashton's eyes glint with tears, and his bottom lip trembles. He holds up his arms to me, and I pick my little tiger up, assuring him that we're all right and safe.

"Take him upstairs. I'll let you know when dinner is ready," Aurielo says.

I open my mouth to object, but he raises his hand, pointing at the stairs.

"Now!" he snaps.

A shiver courses through me as I carry Ashton up the stairs. It's not easy, and I don't dare ask for Aurielo's help or for him to put himself out.

I get it that he's stressed, but it's no way to talk to me. Maybe that shit works with his brother, but I'm not his kin.

I'm his—wife.

Yeah, like that makes a difference.

We're not the least bit equals.

He's the mafia, and I'm his wife. Aurielo married me to protect me, but it doesn't seem like it's working out that way.

We'd be better off getting a divorce. Going our separate ways and never seeing each other again.

My back is sore as hell, but I make it up to the top of the steps. "Ashton, babe. You're getting too big. Can

Mommy put you down?" I should have done that at the bottom of the stairs, but I felt terrible for Ash. The kid has been through hell and doesn't even understand what is going on.

How do I explain it to him?

I can't.

He clutches tighter, and I grumble under my breath the last few steps to his bedroom door. I yank open the door and sit on the edge of the mattress, relieved that his weight is now just in my lap as we sit.

"I want to go home," Ashton whispers. His fingers tangle in my long locks as he keeps his arms snug around my neck.

"I know, babe. I want that too, but for a while, this is going to be our home." Telling him the truth is out of the question. He's too young to understand what I'm doing is to protect him.

But I've failed him.

If Ashton were safe, we never would have been held at gunpoint today.

"Why can't we see Aunt Ivy?" Ashton asks. He shifts to sit beside me on the bed, but he's still clingy, his hands on my arms and hair like if he lets go, I might disappear.

"She's at her house, and we're at our new house. Remember how she used to live in another apartment?" I ask.

Ashton shakes his head no.

He was considerably young when Ivy moved in with us. I shouldn't be surprised that he doesn't remember. She's been bailing my ass out since I got pregnant. Well, she and Jocelyn.

"We didn't always live together. I expected that she'd move out first, though," I say and press a soft kiss to Ashton's temple. I never thought we'd move out and leave her behind.

And I wouldn't have expected that it would have been because I married the man that knocked me up.

Not in a million years would I have bet that I'd have married the stranger.

Even if he is cute.

And sexy.

Not to mention great in bed.

But that one time can't ever happen again. We need to find a way out of this place, away from Aurielo. Because living with him and married to him, we'll never be safe.

## 25

## AURIELO

"You look like shit," Giovan says, coming back into the house after pulling the SUV into the garage and unloading the worn duffel.

My brother never skirts around an issue. Ever. He's always been direct. It's part of the Rinaldi charm.

"Yeah, well, the Bianchis showed up at Gramp's old house." It's still hard for me to refer to the place as my home. Grandpa left me the house instead of Giovan, and it's hard not to feel guilty.

I suggested we sell the place and split the proceeds fifty-fifty, but Giovan told me I was stupid to sell the property. It's been in the family forever. It should stay with the family.

"Etta showed up?"

"No, her father and his crew." I bite down on my bottom lip, tasting blood. "Six of them."

Giovan winces. "He's got surveillance on the old house."

"Obviously." I roll my eyes. How else would we have been seen? The Bianchis aren't quiet people. If they want to be seen, they make it known.

I head into the kitchen, and Giovan follows me. I need to make Ashton and Karina something to eat for dinner. It's getting late, and the kid will be going to bed soon. At least, I assume he will. I have no idea what time he goes to bed.

"What happened? You look like shit, and the kid was shaking when you came inside."

"Yeah, that's the improved version," I say. Watching his tears broke my heart. The only thing I could do was storm inside the house, survey the damage, and refocus my attention.

I don't know a damned thing about being a father, let alone comforting a kid.

But he wasn't looking for me.

He wanted his mom.

"You going to tell me, or do I have to drag your ass outside and beat it out of you?" Giovan asks.

I grumble under my breath as I open the fridge, pulling out staples to make sandwiches for dinner.

"Dorian showed up threatening my family, scaring the kid. He trashed Gramp's house and made it clear that he can kill Karina and Ashton at any time."

Giovan grabs three plates from the opposite cabinet and offers me a hand.

"Your family is safe. You know that Alessandro won't let anything happen to them while they're here."

His words hold little comfort.

"Yeah." I can't lock them up inside the compound. Even if I want to do that, it's not a possibility. Ashton has school, and Karina will never give up her job. But at least she has a bodyguard.

Giovan purses his lips. "I say we take the firefight to him."

"What?" I ask, glancing up from the sandwiches that I'm preparing.

"No one threatens a Rinaldi," Giovan says. "You need to tell Alessandro what happened. He'll order an attack on their home."

I don't want to start a war.

But I don't have a choice. Dorian started this feud, demanding that I marry his kin. "First thing tomorrow," I mutter under my breath.

"Fine, but if you don't tell him, I will," Giovan says.

He's a good brother. Pain in the ass, but he means well.

"You don't have to worry. I'll tell him in the morning." I finish with the sandwiches, grab a handful of potato chips for each plate, and then carry two plates upstairs.

I can't eat. There's a sandwich abandoned on the table for me, but the thought of food turns my stomach.

I bring a tray upstairs, carrying both meals and drinks, and give a firm knock before opening the bedroom door.

Karina is seated on the mattress with Ashton curled up on her lap.

"I brought dinner," I say.

I place the silver tray on a nearby table before flipping on the bedside lamp to add additional light to the room. The sun had set while I was putting dinner together.

I pull the curtains closed, giving the bedroom privacy. Not that anyone can see inside unless they're in the compound.

"Come on," Karina says. She gently pats Ashton's back, trying to untangle him from around her body.

He doesn't dismount from his tight grip around his mother.

"I made sandwiches," I say and step around to glance at Ashton.

Ashton doesn't so much as look at me. His head is turned away, and when I approach, he turns to face away from me.

The kid is mad at me.

I haven't exactly made his life easy, uprooting him, and he hasn't even changed schools yet.

Ashton is going to hate me.

Every kid loves potato chips. "And there's potato chips too. Have you ever put chips in your sandwich?" I ask.

He snorts.

I'm not sure if that's progress or not.

"Ash, babe. I'm going to eat. If you don't want dinner, you can climb under the covers and go to bed," Karina says.

Ashton untangles from Karina and scoots over to sit with her on the bed.

Progress.

I'm pleased when she convinces him to eat, and he quietly sucks down his food faster than I thought a kid possibly could.

He's either starving or avoiding talking, but I'm glad he's getting sustenance.

"Did you eat?" Karina asks.

"I made a sandwich, but it's downstairs," I say. I can't even think of eating. My heart is jackhammering in my chest.

I want to protect my family. I'm just not sure how. Well, other than locking them up inside this room and never letting them leave.

Ashton reaches for a potato chip on his plate and brings it to my lips.

I open my mouth, letting him feed me the salty snack. "Thank you."

He tilts his head slightly, staring at me. "Do you love my mom?" Ashton asks.

The question catches me off guard.

The kid has no idea why he's been whisked from his home, his life, and thrust into this new world. What's the saying? Ignorance is bliss.

Ashton isn't ignorant.

He's innocent. But he's also wise for a five-year-old, which has me worrying more about his well-being than I should be, especially after today's encounter and threat at Gramp's house.

"Your mom is very special to me," I say.

It's not a lie.

She is remarkable. She carried my son. I run my fingers through my hair, flustered. The kid's got my eyes and her smile. He doesn't seem to stop staring at me, which just makes me more nervous.

I'm not used to being around kids.

Let alone my son.

The fact I have a child is bewildering. I still can't wrap my head around it. Another discussion for later, when Ashton is asleep and I have Karina to myself.

But I'm not sure tonight that she'll accompany me in bed, join me in my bedroom, and leave the little guy to sleep alone. If the tables were turned, I wouldn't be able to let him out of my sight.

That bubbling sensation that roars in my belly is unfamiliar.

Worry?

Dread?

I can't put a name to the sensation, but I don't like it. Not at all in the least.

Karina gives a warm smile to Ashton. I can't tell if it's forced or genuine, but she's got dark circles under her eyes.

"How about we get you showered and dressed for bed," Karina says. "Then, it'll be story time before bed."

"Do you have any books?" Ashton asks.

Kids' books, no.

We don't entertain a lot of kids. Hell, Ashton is the first and probably only kid to set foot inside the compound.

"I can check downstairs, but it definitely wouldn't have any pictures in it," I say.

"We don't need a book," Karina says. "There are plenty of stories up in here." She points at her head. "Finish the last of your potato chips and then head into the bathroom to get washed up for bed."

"Fine," Ashton whines.

It's like he's eating his last four potato chips in slow motion, dragging out every bite. The kid sure knows how to stall for bedtime.

I reach for one of his potato chips, and Ashton's eyes widen in horror. He snatches the rest of the chips and shoves them all at once into his mouth before I can steal one from him.

"Careful," I warn. The last thing I want to deal with is a choking kid.

He munches on the last few bites before climbing onto his feet, standing on the mattress, and catapulting off the bed.

"Ashton!" Karina scolds, but he's already in the bathroom and slams the door shut, ignoring his mother. "Sorry about that. He's been through a lot today."

"I'm not upset." Many things trigger me. A kid jumping off the bed isn't one of them.

"Good." She finishes the last bite of the sandwich, and I steal a potato chip from her plate.

Her eyes narrow, but she doesn't steal all the chips and shove them into her mouth like her little boy. She's got more class than that. Although I half expect her to shoo my hand away or chastise me for not eating dinner first. Like a mother would.

"I wanted to talk to you about Ashton."

She visibly swallows, and I reach for a bottle of water that I brought up on the tray, handing it to her.

She takes a sip, washing down her dinner. "He's your son."

Karina confirms my suspicions.

The shower kicks on, which pulls my attention toward the bathroom and then back to Karina.

"I know." I don't need a DNA test to prove the relation. I see it in his eyes and face, the small nose and similar jawline. "After what happened today, I want to enroll him in private school. I think it's for the best, considering that you're living here and driving him to the southside is not only an inconvenience but also a dangerous area. He will have a much better education and upbringing at a private institution nearby."

"You've thought about this for a while?"

She isn't wrong. "Yes, it crossed my mind before our encounter this evening," I say. "But after what transpired, the threat by the Bianchis, I would feel better knowing that he is in the best institution for his education and protected."

"Protected. How?" Karina asks. "Does your mafia own the school?"

I chuckle at her question. "No."

We haven't needed to own a private school, but we own the block and the several streets surrounding the area. The Bianchis are idiots if they step foot anywhere near our turf. "Just trust me, he'll be safe at school."

She purses her lips together but doesn't argue with me.

Does she agree, or is she just too tired to fight and is willing to give in to my demands?

The shower cuts off, and a minute later, I hear his screech. "Mom!" Ashton shouts at the top of his lungs.

The kid could wake the dead.

"Let me grab him pajamas," she says.

It's like she's a mind reader. Maybe she's just intuitive. She knows what the kid needs without him asking. However, his shout was a pretty good indicator of desperation.

Karina digs through the drawers. She's already unpacked his clothes and brings a pair of clean pajamas and undies to the bathroom.

He cracks the door just a few inches and sticks out his hand. She drops the items into his palm before he snatches them and slams the door shut.

The kid certainly knows about privacy. At his age, I was probably still running around naked, not caring about anyone or anything.

He also has a mother who cares about his well-being. My parents would have laughed if I put my hand on the stove. They wouldn't have stopped me.

She comes back to the bed and sits down beside me while Ashton gets dressed. "You were saying?"

It doesn't matter. She seems to agree about sending him to a private school. "Just that I'd like to enroll him in Northshore Academy," I say.

Karina presses her lips tight together. "That's wonderful, but I can't afford to send him to some prestigious school, even without having to pay the rent on my apartment."

The tuition is more than her rent payment. "I'm his father. You don't have to worry about the money. I want what's best for my son."

"That isn't fair. I do, too," Karina says.

"I didn't mean to imply that you don't want what's best for Ashton, just that I can help you afford those things now that I know I have a son."

Her eyes flinch for a second. It's barely noticeable, but I can't tell what she's thinking.

"Are you mad?" she asks.

"About?" I wait for her to continue.

"That I didn't tell you I was pregnant. I know I'd be mad if it were the other way around. I just honestly never thought I'd see you again. We come from different worlds. I would never have run into you if my sister hadn't convinced me to crash the party."

I laugh under my breath, remembering the affair. "Yes, my cousin Nico's engagement party. Francesco wanted to have you taken downstairs to be interrogated."

Her eyes widen. "He would have done that? I thought I was fleeing from the police being called."

She's so innocent and naïve. It's cute.

"We never involve the police."

"Oh." Karina presses her lips tight together. She glances from the bathroom door to the main entrance of the bedroom. "Does he remember me?"

"If you're worried whether he's going to interrogate you now, nearly six years later, you can relax." I don't need her running out of fear of what Francesco might do. He's plenty capable of handling an interrogation, or worse.

The bathroom door flies open, and Ashton hurries for the bed, his wet hair dripping all over the marble floor as he throws himself to the mattress. He climbs to the head of the bed and slips under the covers.

"Story time?" Ashton asks.

"I'm going to grab that sandwich," I say, giving them a moment alone together for a story before bed.

I don't feel right sticking around the bedroom, invading their private ritual. I may be his biological father, but I don't want to intrude. The kid and I barely know one another, and after the hellish day we endured as a family, it's better to let him stick with what he knows.

His mother.

"I'll see you in a bit," Karina says and offers me a faint smile.

I bid goodnight to Ashton before retreating out of the bedroom, shutting the door. I head down the stairs, grabbing the abandoned sandwich on the kitchen counter.

My stomach grumbles as I grab the stool at the counter and take a seat.

Silence fills the void.

Several minutes pass before I hear the soft patter of footsteps and glance over my shoulder at the beauty I'm fortunate enough to be married to. If only she were one hundred percent mine.

"Karina?"

"Ash fell asleep the minute his head hit the pillow. I got as far as 'once upon a time' before he was out cold."

I smile and shake my head, finishing the last bite of my dinner. "Are you still hungry?" I ask. "I can get you something else to eat, dessert?"

Karina steps farther into the kitchen, her feet bare against the marble. "That's okay."

I climb off the stool and grab a bottle of amaretto from the liquor cabinet. It won't be missed. "Play a game with me."

# 26

# AURIELO

I'm not good at small talk or wooing a lady. I've always just managed to get what I want, sex.

With Karina, I want to crack her calm exterior and see what's inside.

It's probably the worst idea and will land my ass into more trouble with her, but I want to loosen us both up.

Alcohol is usually the answer. And if I suggest it as a game, then maybe she'll take the bait.

Her eyes crinkle with a hint of a smile. "That sounds dangerous."

"Good." I grab her hand and drag her back upstairs, this time to our bedroom, alone. I don't need Alessandro or Giovan interrupting us. And I certainly don't want to get dragged into discussing what happened today at the house with the boss.

A good night's sleep will make that easier.

She follows behind me. Her hand latches onto mine. The sensation is warm and strange, unfamiliar, yet I don't want to let go of her, ever.

"What kind of game are we playing that involves alcohol?" Karina asks.

I open the bedroom door and gesture for her to enter first while I flip on the light switch and shut the door, locking it behind me.

No interruptions.

"A drinking game, *Micetta,*" I say.

"We're not twenty anymore," Karina says. "I can't wake up with a hangover. I have work in the morning."

"As do I," I remind her. She's not the only one with responsibilities, and I have to discuss Dorian Bianchi with Alessandro. At least a little alcohol will help me forget about that dreaded moment for a while. "I also want to get Ashton enrolled right away into Northshore Academy, first thing in the morning."

Which means my ass will be up early. But honestly, I don't care. Tomorrow feels like a lifetime away.

She backs up to the bed and props herself on the edge. I kick off my shoes and socks. I should have taken my shoes off when I came into the house, but I'd been distracted with a million other things.

I loosen my tie and pop a few buttons, taking my suit coat off too.

She's trying desperately to hide the grin spreading across her face.

Is she ogling me?

"Like something you see?" I ask, tilting my head as I catch her stare.

She inhales a sharp breath, and her tongue juts out, swiping her top lip. I don't even think she realizes that she makes that small gesture, but it makes my cock hard.

"Just tired. Staring off into space," she says, her voice soft and distant.

Yeah, right.

"Oh, is that so? That's too bad. I thought you were enjoying the show, and I was willing to ditch a few more buttons and maybe even my slacks, but if it's not doing what I thought to you, I can just leave my clothes on."

Karina glances away, her cheeks flaming.

Busted.

I stalk across the empty space between us. I lift her chin, guiding her gaze to mine. "Tell me, *Micetta*. When was the last time that you had sex?"

A soft puff of air spills past her lips. Her eyes darken and her cheeks redden. They're not quite as red as her perfectly cherry lips, but the shade is remarkable. I've never seen her quite so heated, not even when she tried to attack me at the hotel with the lamp.

"That's none of your business," she whispers, staring up at me.

"As your husband, it's my business to know if my wife is being pleased by another man."

She snorts and quips a sideways grin. "You think I'm shacking up at my job? Because that's the only time I don't have your bodyguard on my ass, and I can promise you, Jocelyn isn't my type."

"That's too bad," I tease and lean in closer. Her breath mixes with mine. I want to steal a taste, but I resist the temptation.

Her nose crinkles with a laugh. "You are like every other hot-blooded male out there, imagining two girls together or a threesome."

She isn't wrong.

I would kill to have her in my bed with another woman, but I doubt I can convince her of that, let alone to sleep with me.

Baby steps.

I pull back out of her grasp and open the bottle of amaretto. "Let's play a game," I say, crawling onto the bed beside her.

"I'm listening," she says, her voice soft and sultry.

The girl makes my dick hard.

Part of me knows this is a bad idea. We're married because of Alessandro and not because we want to be. I ought to take things slowly. There's a kid involved, my kid.

But I want to drive myself into her warmth and hear her scream my name. And my senses are lost when she brushes my arm with her gentle touch. Her fingers caress me, and it's not even bare skin.

It's been far too long since I've had a woman in my bed, let alone indulged in a fantasy with one.

Karina isn't the last woman I had sex with. I certainly haven't been a monk for the previous six years, but love hasn't ever been part of the equation. Not that it is now.

I shouldn't kid myself. Just because we're married, doesn't mean we're going to fall happily in love.

This isn't a fairy tale.

This is real life. And real life is filled with flaws and disappointments.

"Give me the bottle," she says when I don't answer her fast enough with how we're going to play the game.

She takes a swig and then screws the lid back on. "How about we play spin the bottle?"

"Are you fourteen?" I joke. There are only two of us, and if she wants to kiss me, she doesn't have to hide behind a game.

I grab her by the waist and pull her against me, our noses bumping together.

We laugh, and she glances down. She's blushing again, brightly.

Reaching for her chin, I guide her head up and our lips brush, taking a taste.

Her mouth is warm and inviting. I pull her onto my lap, desiring more than just a simple kiss. I should have known this was a bad idea.

She doesn't object.

Karina doesn't push me away or tell me to stop.

My fingers glide under her shirt, caressing her lower back, inching her shirt up. I'm slow and meticulous, giving her the opportunity to stop me, to tell me no.

Her moan is like fuel on an already burning fire. She grinds against me, and I deepen the kiss, laying her on her back, straddling her.

I can't keep my hands off her. Not that I'm trying very hard, either.

"Aurielo," she purrs, and my dick stands at attention.

I can't take much more without a sweet release. It's hard to focus, let alone form a complete, coherent sentence. "If you're going to want to stop, we should probably quit now," I say.

"Who said anything about stopping?" Karina asks, staring up at me.

I want to ravish her.

Her fingers work the buttons on my dress shirt free before gliding her palm over my chest and down my stomach, pulling me tighter against her with her legs.

I want this woman.

Not just for tonight.

"Condom?" she asks, still having some semblance of control as I help remove her clothes. I want her naked and writhing beneath me.

I reach for the bedside table and yank hard on the top drawer, retrieving a condom. I strip down but toss the condom on the bed. I'm not ready for it yet.

We've just started, and if I get to have my way with Karina, I intend to take my time and savor every second with this woman.

She's fiery and fierce. Beautiful and stunning. She doesn't even realize the power that she holds over me.

Karina lifts her hips as I guide her pants off and crawl down her torso.

"What are you—" her question is cut off when my lips caress down her stomach for my intended destination. "Oh," she gasps.

Her eyes slam shut. Her fingers tangle in my hair while I lick and suck, teasing her pearl.

I want to drive her over the edge repeatedly.

One orgasm isn't enough. She deserves more. I want her to know that together forever doesn't have to be a prison sentence. In time, we might love one another.

It's a fantasy, a far-fetched one from the reality that we're currently living in, but the thought of another man touching Karina burns me up inside. She hasn't so much as hinted that she's interested in another man, but I don't care.

I must claim her and make her mine.

Not just on paper.

But heart, body, and soul.

She carried my son, my flesh and blood. And I want to do right by her. But letting her leave isn't an option. Don Rinaldi would carry out his threats of murdering both of us.

And that doesn't include the immediate danger that Karina is in because of the Bianchi family. She's a target, and so is my son.

The moans spill past her lips, and I shuck my clothes to the floor, securing the condom before teasing her entrance.

"Are you sure?" I ask, staring down at her, poised at her entrance. I want to fuck Karina more than anything, but I also believe in consent.

Married or not doesn't matter.

It's not like we married because either of us wanted to be.

"Yes, just go slow—it's been a while," she confesses, staring up at me with heavy eyelids.

She's beautiful. A flush has crept across her cheeks and chest, coloring her with desire. Her eyes have darkened, and she arches her back, pulling me closer and deeper.

I cover her lips with mine, giving her all of me.

Karina moans as I fill her.

She's tight and warm. The way she groans my name makes my cock throb.

Each thrust is slow and drawn out, wanting to make this moment last. If I never have tomorrow with her, I want to savor the here and now.

Her moans intensify as I quicken the pace, stroking harder and deeper.

She wraps her legs around me, bringing me tighter inside of her, clenching down as she arches off the mattress.

Her eyes are slammed shut.

"Look at me," I command. I don't even know why the words spill out my lips. I've never made Etta or the dozens of other women look at me when they come. Usually, I roll them over, blast into them from behind, refusing to meet their intense stare.

With Karina, it's different.

She's different.

She isn't any of those girls.

Her lips part, and she no longer silences her moans as she tightens onto my shaft, trembling and pulsating.

The sensation is overwhelming.

My heart slams against my chest, begging to break free.

I cover her lips with mine. She's eager, her kiss strong and fierce, tongues dueling together as I finally shudder and release into her before collapsing above her.

Reluctantly, I pull out and remove the condom, taking it into the bathroom to discard. Grumbling, I realize the condom broke somewhere between putting it on and removing it.

The bedroom is dark, but I know my way around the room.

She shuffles on the bed, and in another minute I'm back on the mattress, pulling the covers up around us.

I need to tell her, but my stomach is in knots.

We already have one kid.

Can we handle two?

I wrap my arms around her waist and pull her against me. "*Micetta*," I whisper.

Karina doesn't pull away. She mumbles something unintelligible. Already, she's drifting to sleep.

It's not like there's anything we can do about it tonight.

Curling around her, I close my eyes, but I can't relax. My fingers itch to touch her stomach, caress her skin, and imagine what it would be like if she was pregnant with my child again.

# 27

# KARINA

The alarm jars me awake. I groan and realize Aurielo's warm body is nestled tight against me.

Naked.

Did that really happen last night?

I can't just sneak out. The alarm is blaring, which means he's probably awake too. But he hasn't budged an inch.

Reluctantly, I pull back from his embrace and climb out of bed, stealing the sheet to give me a little modesty.

"You look better naked," Aurielo says.

"I knew you were awake." I glance over my shoulder at him as I make my way to the dresser. He's left me two drawers on the bottom and half of his closet, which is more than I expected. He also mentioned another dresser being delivered to the bedroom, but I'm not sure if he means that a new one was purchased or another piece of furniture is being shuffled around the mansion.

I grab a quick change of clothes and hurry into the bathroom. I can't afford to be late again this week.

The dragon will breathe fire down my neck and roast me.

Maybe I deserve it a little.

It's not like I've been myself lately. Sleeping with Aurielo is not one of my proudest moments. But I can't compare what I did with him nearly six years ago to what happened last night.

I pinch the bridge of my nose and stare at my reflection in the bathroom mirror.

"Who are you?" I whisper. I don't even recognize myself.

I dress as quickly as possible and hurry out of the bathroom.

"Can we talk?" Aurielo asks.

My stomach flops. Is he about to tell me that he regrets sleeping with me and wants to start seeing other people even though we're married?

It's not like we married out of desire. It wasn't a choice.

Well, not much of a choice. Death, or marry the mobster.

I chickened out and took the marriage route. Maybe I should have let him put a bullet in me and end my life. But wouldn't that have been more selfish for Ashton? Perhaps it was selfish for me because Ashton's life was in danger. If I were dead, he'd be safe.

"I have to head into work," I say, avoiding what happened and talking.

I hate the 'we have to talk' speech. It never goes well. Ever.

"I'll enroll Ashton this morning," Aurielo says.

"You don't mind?" I head for the door. I need to leave now if I want to make it into the city on time. Usually, I drop Ashton at school early before work, and he's part of an early morning program that keeps the kids busy and entertained in the school gymnasium until classes start.

If I depended on Ivy to get him to school, he wouldn't roll in until around lunchtime. Maybe an hour earlier.

"It's not a problem," Aurielo says. "Do I call his current school to get his information transferred over?"

"I'll call as soon as I get into work and have them fax his transcripts. I mean, the kid is in kindergarten. How much paperwork can there be on him?"

He sits up in bed and runs a hand through his dark hair. "I'll likely need his birth certificate and social security number," Aurielo says.

"I can ask Ivy to drop those items off at his new school." I open the bedroom door. If I leave now, I can still make it to work on time.

————

"Someone got laid," Jocelyn says, glancing me over in the breakroom.

I fill my water bottle and take a swig.

How the hell can she tell? "Is it that obvious?" I laugh nervously. I'm not ready for her assault of twenty questions.

"Well, you *are* married, and since you didn't go on a honeymoon, I just assumed you're christening every surface in your new abode. Are you two living together at his place or yours?" she asks.

Jocelyn isn't the least bit subtle with her questions, but at least she isn't asking me in front of the patients. Especially since our patients are kids, that would be highly inappropriate.

"His place, uptown," I say, not giving anything further away. He lives a little more than just 'uptown.' He's outside of the city in a residential area that is still heavily congested, more so than the typical suburbs. It's barely outside of the city.

"You are so cryptic," Jocelyn says and grabs a soda from the fridge. She pops the drink open and pulls the tab right off without a second thought. "He is

handsome. You sure know how to pick the hotties."
She pauses and takes a sip of her drink.

"Hotties?" I repeat.

"Yes," she says, staring at me like I'm an idiot.

"I'm not sure what you mean by hotties, as in plural."
I fold my arms across my chest defensively. I haven't
slept with anyone since that night when Ashton was
conceived. Well, until last night.

"You didn't tell me you were dating, let alone serious
with anyone. What is up with that?" Jocelyn stares
me down, waiting for an explanation.

I don't have one. Not one that I intend to give her.

I'm trying to protect her by keeping her far away
from Aurielo and his men. Especially after what
happened last night at his home up north. Ashton
could have been shot, or worse, killed.

"It's complicated," I say and shuffle my feet, trying to
avoid her intense gaze.

It doesn't work.

Jocelyn steps closer.

"Come on, talk to me. We're practically family," Jocelyn says.

"I can't. I'm trying to protect you." That's the last word I intend to have about Aurielo, the marriage, and my sex life with her. It's all off the table. Anything else is fair game; the weather, Ashton, even my sister's love life, I'll gossip about. But not the mafia or how I ended up in this situation.

"You know I'm going to get it out of you," Jocelyn says. She takes a swig of her cold soda, the outside perspiring from the air. I feel like that can, under her scrutiny and sweating immensely.

Except I'm not physically sweating.

But emotionally, I'm a wreck. I bite down on my bottom lip to subdue the urge to run. Where would I go? How far would I get?

It'd be easier to bolt out of the breakroom and away from Jocelyn, which is what I do. "I have to get back to work," I say and skirt past her.

Her eyes narrow as she watches me leave the room.

She's going to nag the crap out of me until I give her some juicy details. That's just how Jocelyn is with things. Maybe if I feed her little bits of the truth, just enough of a taste to make her leave me alone, that will suffice.

Truthfully, though, I want someone to confide in about what I'm going through. Ivy is the most practical person to reach out to, but I don't want to endanger her life, either. And after what happened yesterday, going it alone seems the safest option.

I head in to check on Molly Ryan. She's a sweet kid. She just turned six last week.

"Nurse Karina!" Molly squeals, and her eyes light up. She cuddles her fluffy white unicorn with a rainbow mane. "Look what Mommy gave me for my birthday."

Her excitement spills over like a river's bank. Even with all that she's endured, the kid is strong and one hell of a fighter.

"Have you given her a name?" I ask. I check Molly's vitals and jot down the information on her chart.

"Tallulah." Molly beams with excitement. "Isn't she so pretty? And she still has all her hair!"

I chuckle, glad that Molly can take what she's going through and still find a reason to smile.

Some days, I force myself to be happy while I'm on the job. While chipper isn't usually one of my moods, I can't let what's happening affect the patients.

And that includes my home life issues.

It took years for me to learn to compartmentalize what happens at work and leave the job behind when I go home for the day. Constantly focusing on the fact that I work with sick and dying children isn't a picnic.

Don't get me wrong, the job is rewarding, but emotionally, it's also physically draining. And having my own son at home, it's challenging when he shows me a bump on his head, for me not to worry that it could be something more than a nasty spill.

Do I overreact?

Yes.

Am I a helicopter parent?

Probably.

I try not to be. I do my best to give Ashton his freedom, as much as I can, and let him experience the world as he should.

But it's hard watching kids suffer. The joy in the job is being there for those children, helping them, tending to them, being their anchor of support.

And with kids like Molly, with her bright, infectious smile, it's hard not to smile back. She's a sweetheart.

"I want hair just like Tallulah's."

I force a smile.

Molly is wearing an orange and red scarf with poppies decorating the fabric. I don't recall her ever being on the pediatric unit with hair. She was a transfer from another hospital outside the city. Her parents relocated for her treatment.

"You want rainbow hair?" I ask. I'd surmise she probably just wants hair of any kind that's not falling out and thin from the chemotherapy.

"Do you think you can ask Mom to get me a rainbow wig?" Molly grins. "I know my birthday just passed, but I wish I had rainbow hair!"

"I'll see what I can do," I say and give her a wink. "How are you feeling today?" I ask, checking the IV drip.

A code blue is called over the loudspeaker on our floor. My stomach tenses, and I muster the best smile that I can to Molly.

"I'll be right back."

I hurry out of the room and to the patient's room to assist in the code blue.

My feet pound against the ground, rushing as fast as I can across the corridor and down the hallway to the opposite side of the floor.

It's Cora's room.

Fourteen-year-old Cora Clarke.

Rushing inside, I see that her skin is ghastly. She's lying flat on the bed, her pillow removed.

Jocelyn is doing chest compressions while another staff member rushes in a crash cart to assist.

The room spins. I step out into the hall, more importantly, out of the way. I don't want to be a burden.

Sweat trickles down my forehead. I'm going to be sick.

———

The day goes from bad to worse.

The elevator dings at the nurse's station, and I glance up, expecting Cora's parents to come and say their goodbyes.

She didn't make it.

I still have to call the morgue and have them retrieve the body and bring it down to the basement.

Francesco steps out onto the pediatric unit. "What are you doing on our floor? No visitors."

I'm not in the mood to deal with his antics, or Alessandro's, for that matter. I doubt Aurielo gave him orders to stalk me at my job.

"Change of plans," Francesco says. "You're done your shift."

I glance at the clock. "I'm almost done. There are twenty more minutes." I'm not leaving early because the baboon tells me I'm finished.

"We need to get back to the house, now," he snarls at me.

Jocelyn comes jetting around the corner and nearly stumbles right into Francesco. She stops herself mid-stride.

Her face is red, splotchy. She's been crying.

We've all been dealing with Cora's death in different ways.

Me?

I bottle that shit up.

It's not necessarily the most healthy, but it's the only way I know how to process death.

"Are you taking off?" Jocelyn asks.

"Yes," Francesco answers for me.

I open my mouth to say no, but he pins me with his gaze. "Aurielo wants you home."

"Let me get changed, and I'll be right out." I exhale a heavy sigh and head down the hall to get changed.

Jocelyn is on my heel a second later. "What's with him?" she asks, keeping her voice low.

"What do you mean?" I open my locker, slip out of my sneakers, and strip down out of my scrubs, changing into casual wear, black yoga pants and an extra comfy t-shirt. Even my clothes are beginning to smell like Aurielo.

"I've seen him in the lobby almost every day. I'm pretty sure every day that you're working."

Jocelyn's gone out to lunch far more often than I do, especially with Francesco playing bodyguard. I've avoided leaving the floor until my shift is over.

"He works with Aurielo. A hired bodyguard." I hold up a hand. "Don't make a big deal about it. Okay?"

"Why do you need a bodyguard?" Jocelyn asks.

The girl never stops with the questions. She's as inquisitive as Molly, but at least on a six-year-old it's endearing.

"I don't know, Aurielo could be worth money. His job is super influential and prestigious. Maybe he's secretly a billionaire?" I'm trying to distract her from the obvious fact that Francesco looks like a mobster with his dark suit, thick black hair, and the Italian accent to boot.

"You don't know why he has the Hulk follow you around, do you?" Jocelyn quips.

I slip on my shoes and slam the locker shut. "His name is Francesco," I correct her. I'm not sure why I'm defending him. He's been bossy and overbearing. The man is a million times worse to deal with than Aurielo.

At least there's a physical attraction between Aurielo and myself, which was made evident last night in the bedroom. The room feels several degrees hotter, and I slip past Jocelyn, heading for the open door.

"There's a lot I can't tell you, Jocelyn. I wish I could, but it's safer if you don't ask quite so many questions."

Her eyes flinch as she watches me head down the hallway.

I hope I didn't bring more tears to her eyes, but I must separate my work from personal life. It's the only way to survive.

"Let's go," I say to Francesco and hit the down button for the elevator.

"Rough day?" he asks as the elevator dings.

The double doors open. Cora's parents step out onto the floor.

I swallow the bile rising in my throat and choke back the sob that wants to form.

Bury the pain.

Swallow the emotions.

It's a mantra I silently chant in my head.

I don't know how long it will work as I step into the elevator before it all explodes and brings me to my knees.

Right now, I'm numb.

Everything inside of me aches. I want nothing more than to go home.

But Aurielo's place isn't home. There's no warmth and comfort in the unfamiliar.

It's torture.

## 28

## KARINA

I head inside, and Francesco ushers me upstairs to Ashton's room.

"What's going on? Where's Aurielo?" I don't like the silence or the fact I'm being manhandled and given orders.

That's not what I signed up for.

Not that I wanted any of this, but Francesco is supposed to protect me, not boss me around the house. Who the hell does he think he is?

"Aurielo is busy working," Francesco says with a grunt. "Get in the bedroom and don't leave until one of us comes to get you."

He yanks the door open, and I'm surprised he doesn't rip it off its hinges with the amount of force he uses.

Ashton is sitting on the floor with several toy trains, playing quietly.

I flip on the overhead light. The window shades are open, but the room isn't particularly bright at this time of day. The sun is shining on the opposite side of the mansion.

"Did you go to school today?" I ask.

Aurielo was supposed to enroll him at the private school. I had the paperwork sent over, along with the necessary documents and anything else he might have required.

"Yes." Ashton presses his lips together, his brow tight.

"How was it?" I ask and come to sit on the floor beside him.

I need a distraction from my shitty day.

He shrugs.

That's not the type of response that I was envisioning. "Did you go to a new school?" I ask.

Ashton nods and glances up at me. "I had to wear a stupid uniform."

"Did the other kids at the school wear the same uniform?" I ask. I can't imagine that he was singled out, but it's certainly not something he's been accustomed to doing.

Ashton has been picking out his clothes, even at the store when we go shopping. He doesn't care if he wears mismatched socks or plaid pants with a striped shirt.

And I'm not the fashion police. Whatever makes him happy and wearing his clothes and being independent is a big part of that, but so is following the rules.

He doesn't answer me.

"I know you're not crazy about your new school, but I'll bet if you give it time, you'll make lots of new friends." I want him to get a better education. It'll help him in the long run, not that he understands any of that now. But this opportunity, it's huge for him.

"I want to go home," Ashton says.

I exhale a heavy sigh. "I know, but this is our home now." I wish I could explain it to him, but I don't know how to tell a five-year-old the truth without telling him all the scary stuff that we've been entangled in by a simple mistake.

Besides, he shouldn't shoulder that type of burden.

He's a kid.

"Can we play outside?" Ashton asks, putting his truck down on the floor.

"Not right now," I say. I'm honestly not sure why we've been sequestered to the bedroom. It seems a little like overkill.

Is Aurielo punishing us for some reason?

Is it because we slept together, and I rushed out this morning without doing as he asked, talking?

This is my fault. It has to be.

When isn't screwing up a relationship on me? I'm bad at relationships.

"Please," Ashton whines. "It's for school. The teacher gave us homework."

"What do you have to do outside?" I ask.

"We're supposed to count how many different colors we see in one area."

There isn't much room to roam freely, except for the garden. "Okay." I concede. If the kid has a homework assignment, who am I to stop him?

He's at a new school with new teachers. The last thing I need is for Ashton to fall behind.

"Grab your assignment," I say and stand.

He reaches for his schoolbag and pulls out a sheet of paper and pencil.

"We have to be quiet. Okay?" I remind him. I don't need to run into Francesco or anyone else if I can help it.

Ash follows my lead out of the bedroom and down the hallway. I'm careful to be quiet and make my footsteps invisible.

Thankfully, Ashton isn't being overly zealous or his usual chatty carefree self. Maybe he realizes the importance of following my instruction?

Doubtful.

We quietly sneak down the stairs, through the long corridor, and to the French doors that lead to the garden.

He runs outside, foregoing shoes and socks. The kid is going to be a mess later.

I shut the doors without so much as a click of the lock as I stroll into the garden with my son. He's already cataloging and jotting down all the details for his assignment.

I head across the stones for the swing.

It's broken, knocked over, and unusable.

What happened in here?

Retreating my steps, I glance around, ensuring that it's just the two of us and we're alone. I don't spot anyone else in the garden, not that I've seen anyone frequent the area in the couple of days that I've been at the mansion.

Ashton fills up the sheet of paper front and back before throwing himself down onto the grass, staring up at the sky.

The sun is setting, and it casts a warm, orange glow across the sky. I find an empty space and take a seat.

A male voice clears his throat.

I glance behind me at the figure looming near the door. I hadn't heard anyone come into the garden.

"You need to be inside, upstairs."

The man is older, rougher, and unrefined. I recognize him from the hotel room, Alessandro. He's the boss around here and the one who ordered me killed.

Ashton has finished his assignment. "Yes, of course."

I don't argue. There's no need.

He's a man not to be messed with, and he's allowed my son to live here with me.

Ashton climbs to his feet. I stand, taking my son's hand, keeping him close.

Alessandro yanks the French doors open and waits for us to trudge inside before shutting the glass doors and escorting us to the staircase.

I'm surprised he doesn't walk us both up to the room that we've been sequestered to, but perhaps taking the stairs is a little too far out of his way. We've inconvenienced him. I can feel the energy and anger sizzling beneath the surface. At least he knows how to hold his tongue, especially in front of my child.

I open the bedroom door and let Ashton inside.

Where's Aurielo? If he's at work, why is Alessandro giving orders for us to hide up in the bedroom?

Something feels amiss.

Is it because of the attack yesterday and the threats of those men? Aren't we supposed to be safe here?

It'll be time for dinner soon enough, and I can't imagine we'll be forced to eat in the bedroom or, worse, go without dinner.

Aurielo wouldn't be that cruel to his son. Would he?

"Can you color me a picture?" I ask Ashton.

I want to distract him while I have a look around.

## 29

### AURIELO

We hadn't been able to nab Don Bianchi, but snagging his second in command, Matteo, is no less a victory.

He's tied up on a chair in the basement, in a holding cell.

Imprisoned.

He's awaiting my interrogation.

Alessandro has already given me command over the situation. Being too close to a criminal can be all-consuming. But I want Matteo to feel the same dread and trepidation that I experienced last night at his boss's hands.

I stomp down the stairs and pause. Giovan is standing guard outside Matteo's prison cell. Not that we anticipate him escaping, but you can never be too careful.

We're more concerned that he might hang himself or find another way to commit suicide and avoid an extensive and excruciating interrogation.

Giovan pulls me aside, his voice low so the monster can't hear what's being said.

"Are you sure you're up for this?" Giovan asks.

I cast a quick glance at Matteo and then back at Giovan. "Are you suggesting that I'm incapable of keeping a level head?"

He cracks a grin. Giovan would never suggest such a thing. He would, however, remind me not to go easy on a criminal whom we've captured.

And I have no intent on being generous or kind. We're not cops or feds. There's no jurisdiction or code of honor bullshit to worry about. It's what makes my methods infallible.

"I'm sure his good looks or charisma won't sway you," Giovan jokes.

A smile doesn't reach my lips.

Although I feel relieved that we caught Matteo, how we got to him, I wasn't part of the mission. I'd been too busy enrolling Ashton into kindergarten at the private school.

If I had been on hand for the takedown, I'd have put a bullet in Matteo's head. He'd have never made it to the compound for an interrogation.

Another set of heavy footsteps resonate down the stairs.

I glance over my shoulder at Francesco.

He gives me a nod. Everything is fine. Karina and Ashton are upstairs, safe. I called him the moment I found out I had an interrogation to handle. The last thing I want is Karina getting wind of what we're doing.

Knowing and seeing are two completely different things.

"You need help with him?" Francesco asks. "A little muscle to beat the truth right out of him? It's been a few days since I got my hands dirty."

Francesco doesn't even sugarcoat it.

He wants blood for blood. The Bianchis threatened Karina and Ashton, my family, which is a threat directly to the Rinaldi family.

I want Matteo dead.

———

Blood drips from my knuckles as I slam my fist into Matteo's jaw.

It's not the least bit of a fair fight, with his arms tied behind his back and restrained to a chair.

No one said anything we ever did was fair or honorable.

The kind thing to do would be to put the bastard out of his misery.

End his life.

I'm not generous.

I'm a savage.

"I'm not telling you a damned thing," Matteo says and spits in my face.

I move out of the way, but his spit lands on my shirt.

Fucking asshole.

He laughs.

The darkness invades my soul.

I slam my fist against his face and across his nose. I can feel the bones break and hear the crunch that sends a shudder down my spine.

I swallow the disgust and anger. The revolting vileness that seeps out from this man and onto me.

He's given me no choice but to be this way, to torture him until he's executed.

"You threaten my family. You can expect to pay the price," I say.

His head hangs low, and blood drips from his nose onto the cement floor, puddling below.

"I have nothing," Matteo says. He glances up with darkened eyes and a sinister smile. "Nothing to lose."

"I suppose your life is pretty worthless." I agree. It doesn't mean I intend to spare him pain or suffering.

"Tell me what Dorian is planning. He shouldn't give a damn about who I marry. Etta and I ended things months ago."

For years, we'd been on-again and off-again with some semblance of a relationship. It was purely physical. Sexual. And she had a wandering eye in the end, which made me cut all ties to her and end any idea of a relationship or marriage between us.

"Dorian wants to mend the girl's broken heart," Matteo says.

Yeah, I don't buy that for a second.

"Dorian only cares about himself." If he cared about anyone else, he'd have sent men after us to retrieve Matteo.

Instead, Matteo is being sacrificed. The Bianchis aren't coming to save him. Even if they wanted to, we're in a fortress guarded by dozens of men with guns. They're not getting inside.

"True," Matteo says, his voice gravelly and weak.

I don't fall for his routine, the one where he pretends to be near death and in agony, only to fight back. I've seen it time and time again amongst cowards.

"He does want you dead. You, Alessandro, the entire family."

I pull up a spare wooden chair and flip it around to sit, my arms folded across the top. "That's not news. Our families have been feuding for as long as I can remember. Even as a kid. You have to give me more than that, Matteo. You're not Dorian's second without knowing what's going on inside his head. If you don't value your own life, maybe you value your family?" I ask.

Silence encompasses the room.

"Nothing?" I tsk and shake my head. "That's a shame. I was hoping we could put the torture behind us and move straight to your untimely death."

Matteo's eyes flash up at me as he winces. "You won't kill me."

"Won't I?" What makes him so sure that I'll let him leave? He was there yesterday, threatening my family with Dorian and on Dorian's orders.

"You'll start a war between our families."

If this is his way of begging to be kept alive, it's not the least bit working on me.

"I hate to break it to you, but the war's already been started."

I slam my fist against his face, unpleased with his answer. My knuckles are bloody, but I ignore the slight pain.

Besides, the blood is entirely his.

"I can go all night," I warn. "What is Dorian planning? He didn't show up just to threaten my wife and the boy."

I refrain from naming Ashton as my son, especially in front of this monster. He doesn't get to discover that the child is my son.

There's a soft feminine gasp from the opposite side of the prison bars near the stairwell.

Fuck!

I glance over my shoulder and catch sight of Karina.

She gasps and hurries back up the stairs.

Francesco chases after her. His footsteps thunder above.

Matteo grins, his lips bloody and his left eye swollen. "Let me guess. The new wife doesn't know what you do for a living?" A darkened laugh spills past his lips, his shoulders sagging forward. He coughs and spits. Redness lands on my arm.

I wipe the spit away and pummel him in the chest, knocking his chair backward and onto the floor.

Standing, I tower over him, my foot crushing against his lungs. "Giovan!" I shout for my brother.

He unlocks the prison door. "If he won't talk tonight, we'll continue tomorrow with the interrogation. Ever have a tooth pulled?" I ask.

It's a rhetorical question.

We have a vast selection of tools from pliers, car batteries, to pruning shears. I prefer to use my fists and beat the hell out of a guy before we take things up a notch. Torture usually encourages them to tell you anything. Not necessarily the truth. They just want the pain to stop.

I'm a bit old school.

A beat-down loosens them up for the harsher shit.

I'd rather the bastard spill the truth now. It'd save us both a bunch of time and his suffering, but they never go the easy route.

I head out of the prison cell, letting Giovan lift Matteo's chair and put him back in a sitting position, tied to the chair, before locking the metal doors, leaving the prisoner alone.

Giovan follows behind me up the stairs.

"That was Karina who snuck down here. Wasn't it?" Giovan asks.

I was hoping he didn't notice. But that's impossible given how Francesco chased Karina up the stairs.

"Yeah, one more thing to deal with tonight." I remove my shirt on the way upstairs. Covered in blood and Matteo's spit, I need a shower.

"Can't wait to get your clothes off for that hottie wife of yours," Giovan jokes.

I step onto the main floor landing and wait for him to join me before slamming the basement door shut and locking it with the reinforced double deadbolts.

"Watch your mouth," I warn. "You want to have your face looking like Matteo's?"

Giovan holds his hands up in surrender. "Understood."

I slip out of my shoes and stalk up the stairs to the bedroom.

Francesco stands outside my door. "Is Karina in there?" I ask.

He gives a sneer and a jab at the door. "Yeah. The kid's in his room. I thought I ought to separate her for a while. Let her see what it's like to be in her own little prison."

Alessandro undoubtedly got wind of her sneaking down to the basement prison. If he didn't know about it, Francesco sure as hell announced it with him chasing her upstairs to the bedroom.

So much for subtlety.

"I'll keep an eye on her," I offer. I've got to clean up and shower anyhow. As long as I'm in the same room with her, I might as well let Francesco have a break. The guy's been guarding her since early this morning at work.

"Boss's orders are that I remain outside her room and stand guard."

I don't argue with Francesco. He's a big guy, and I'm in desperate need of a hot shower and change of clothes.

"Have at it," I say, stepping past him as I open the bedroom door.

Karina is seated on the bed, her arms folded across her chest. She glances up, her eyes widening when she sees me, and then her shoulders slump.

Was she expecting someone else?

I undo my belt, pulling it off and leaving it on the top of the dresser while I rummage around for a pair of jeans, boxers, and a t-shirt. I take the items into the bathroom and turn around before shutting the door to face her.

"You need to use the bathroom?" I ask.

She shakes her head no.

I shut the bathroom door and turn on the shower spray before stripping down.

The smell of blood is mixed with sweat. I wait until the shower is hot before stepping under the stream.

Dirt, grime, and blood swirl down the drain as the hot water pounds over me.

A cool gust of air fills the bathroom.

"Karina?" Who else would interrupt me?

"Did you kill him?" she asks.

The shower curtain is the only semblance of privacy, not that she seems to care. "Do you want the truth?" I ask, half expecting her to yank it open and demand to know what happened.

"I don't want you to lie to me!" Her voice raises an octave. "That man, from yesterday, he wants my son and me dead. I can't sleep knowing he's in the same house as us."

Her voice is laced with fear and uncertainty. Anxiety is creeping in and rearing its ugly head. I pull open the shower curtain and reach for her.

"What are you doing?" she asks. "You're getting me wet."

I snicker at her response. "That's the point. A hot shower is a good way to unwind." Among other activities.

"Aurielo." Karina hesitates, her eyes wide. She's holding back.

Is she afraid of me?

I drop my wet hands from her arms. I won't force her to do anything.

Hasn't she realized that yet? Unless it's for her health or safety.

"I'll be done in a few minutes," I say and shut the shower curtain, ducking my head back under the spray.

I'd have like to have devoured her and enjoyed some mind-blowing shower sex, but clearly, she wasn't in the mood. Not that interrogating and beating a guy up in the basement prison gets me horny. Because it doesn't.

But being around Karina makes me do things that I wouldn't ordinarily do. Like fuck a stranger.

I've had my share of one-night stands but never in the middle of a party, in the office, with a woman I've never met before. That was crazy, even by my standards.

I finish in the shower, step out, and dry off. After I get dressed, I open the bathroom door.

She's back on the bed as if she hadn't just come into the bathroom moments earlier.

"We need to talk," I reiterate. I'm not sure now is the best time to reveal to her that the condom broke last night, but she needs to know at some point and probably before nine months pass.

Not that I anticipate a baby.

I don't.

It's probably fine, as long as she's not ovulating.

"Talk? I swear, I won't go down there again. I didn't know what you were doing or where you were. Alessandro caught us outside in the garden and ordered Ashton and me to his bedroom."

"You should have listened to him, *Micetta*." I don't like that she disobeyed a direct order from the boss.

She stares down at her hands in her lap. "I wish I would have. Can I stay with Ashton? He's in his room all alone. He's probably worried about me."

Her concern is genuine, but Francesco isn't going to let her see her son. And I'm sure it's on Alessandro's orders.

"He'll be fine. How about I go in and check on him?" I say. "He's probably getting hungry for dinner too."

She chews on her bottom lip. Like she wants to say something but is holding back.

"What?" I ask. It's hard to read a woman I barely know.

I want to get to know her, every inch of her body and her mind, but she's making it difficult for me. Not that she cares. She's used to living in her perfect world with freedom and little consequence.

The mafia world isn't like that.

You cross someone, and you end up dead.

Did she learn nothing from the hotel?

I want to protect her, but she needs to be vigilant and cautious. She can't go traipsing through the compound. Although I'm sure from now on, a guard will be stationed outside her room when she's home from work.

"It's been a rough day," she says.

I raise a curious eyebrow. Is she referring to the man she watched me assault in prison or something else? "Is everything all right with Ashton?" My stomach somersaults just thinking that he could have had a difficult first day at his new school.

I wanted to see how his day went, if he made any new friends, but I'd been caught up with work that while I had picked him up, I'd been on the phone the entire time with Alessandro.

"Aside from hating the school uniforms, yeah, he's fine," Karina says.

I exhale a breath, relieved at least he's still all right. The kid had been through an ordeal last night back at my house. I hadn't expected any of it to go down as it had. I'd wanted to show Karina the life that we could have outside the compound. I just needed time to convince Alessandro that I don't need to live on site and that he can trust us.

But after the place was destroyed and our lives threatened, I don't want us to live anywhere else. Karina and Ashton's safety is my priority, and I can only ensure they're protected inside the compound.

She presses her lips together. "We can talk later." Karina gestures for the door. "Go check on my son, please."

"Our son," I correct her, heading for the bedroom door. "I'll bring you dinner."

I don't imagine that Alessandro is going to allow her to leave the bedroom tonight. He might not for the next week except to leave for work.

His punishments may seem harsh, but he's trying to protect her. And I agree with Alessandro. Karina should never have come down to the basement. The prison is entirely off-limits.

Thankfully, she was smart enough not to bring Ashton with her.

"I doubt I can eat," Karina says. "No rush."

"There's a book on the nightstand if you want something to do," I say.

"I swear if it's the Bible—"

I snort at her comment. "Is that a joke?" I honestly can't tell if she's being serious or trying to make light of the situation. "It's a political thriller. But I swear if you spoil the ending," I tease her, "you will have to face my wrath."

She chews on her bottom lip. "Then I guess I'll have to keep it a secret."

I'll bet she's good at keeping secrets. She kept the fact she was pregnant with my child hidden from me.

Though in her defense, she didn't know who I was. But she also didn't try to find me, either.

———

After dinner with Ashton, I let him sneak into our bedroom to give his mom a hug goodnight.

Francesco isn't pleased, but Karina isn't leaving the room.

No rules are broken.

Right?

"Thank you," she whispers to me as I lead Ashton back to his bedroom for bed. I don't have a story to read to him, but his head hits the pillow, and he's already closing his eyes to sleep.

I'll take that as a win.

I hurry downstairs, grab Karina's dinner, and bring it up to the bedroom. It's a few minutes after eight, and she's probably starving.

Brushing past Francesco standing guard, I head for the bedroom. "I'm in for the night," I say. He doesn't need to stand guard twenty-four hours a day.

But if Alessandro tells him to jump off a bridge, the man would do it.

Francesco concedes and heads down the hall for his bedroom.

I slip into my room, shut the door behind me, the tray of food in hand as I bring it over to the bed.

"Hungry?"

Karina glances up from the book that I loaned her. She dog ears the page and places it on the nightstand.

"No. I don't think I can stomach anything."

"Well, you need to eat," I say.

Did she lose her appetite with what she witnessed in the basement with the prisoner?

It takes time to feel nothing when it comes to torturing a man. I'd worry if it didn't bother her.

"I'll feed you myself if I have to, *Micetta*," I warn.

# 30

# KARINA

I say nothing, force myself to eat a few bites of dinner, and then climb under the covers without a word.

There's nothing Aurielo can say that can fix what happened.

He brutally beat a man.

While I don't know why, I suspect it had to do with what happened yesterday.

An eye for an eye doesn't get anyone anywhere. Aurielo and his men aren't above that type of behavior.

It'd be a lie if I said I wasn't terrified of the Bianchi family and the threat they made on my son and myself. But being in the Rinaldi home doesn't seem any better.

I have to get out before it's too late.

I lie in bed. The sun hasn't even risen from the horizon yet, but I can't sleep. I do my best not to toss and turn. I don't want to wake the savage who's sound asleep beside me.

Is there still a guard posted outside the bedroom door?

I'm tempted to tiptoe across the room, sneak to the door, and pry it open. But what would I even do? Escape with Ashton in the middle of the night, to where exactly?

Ashton isn't a baby. It's harder to escape with a curious five-year-old than a sleeping infant. Not to mention, carrying him isn't my first choice.

I need a plan.

The clock ticks by, and each second, it matches my pulse. I expect the clock to beat faster as my fear grips me from the inside out.

I have to make Aurielo believe that I'm not afraid of him.

He needs to feel that he can trust me and grant me freedom, and when he does, I'll take the opportunity and run with Ashton.

But I'll need help.

I can't return to my apartment. That's the first place that Aurielo will come looking for me. I could ask Jocelyn for help, but Aurielo isn't stupid. He'll interrogate anyone I worked with or I'm friends with, and I don't want him treating Jocelyn like he did that man in the basement.

Even if the Bianchis are monsters, that doesn't mean Aurielo needs to be one. There has to be another way to get what he wants without involving torture.

---

Work is somber.

There's a heaviness that extends amongst the staff after Cora's death.

I glance in at Cora's empty room. Her belongings were cleaned out and taken home by her parents.

The pictures on the walls that she drew have been removed. It's stark and empty. It smells of antiseptic.

Another patient hasn't taken over the room yet.

But they will, and all I can hope is that their outcome is better.

Happier.

I sneak off during a break and grab the burner phone that my sister gave me.

She picks up on the first ring.

"Where are you? Is everything okay?" Ivy asks.

No.

Nothing is okay.

"I'm at work," I rasp. My voice catches in my throat. "I need your help."

"Whatever it is, I'm here for you."

Ivy isn't the most dependable person, but she will throw her life on the line for her nephew and me when it comes to sisterhood.

I give her a brief overview of the last few days with Aurielo, the Bianchis, and then what I witnessed last night.

"Shit, you really are in with the mafia," Ivy says. "Tell me what you need. Papers? A place to escape to outside the city?"

"All of it," I whisper, careful to keep my voice down.

"I'll see what I can do," Ivy says. "Keep Ashton close. If that lunatic lays a finger on my nephew—"

"He won't," I say, interrupting her. I shut the door to the breakroom, making sure no one can overhear the conversation. "Ashton is Aurielo's son. He's not going to let anything happen to his kid. Which is why I need to get us out now before things get more complicated."

"Fuck. I worried something was going on between the two of you," Ivy says.

Whatever we had is over.

This isn't the conversation I want to be having with Ivy, and certainly not over the phone. "Can you help me or not?" I glance at my watch. I'm running out of time.

My break is over.

Any minute, Jocelyn or one of the other nurses or staff members will come looking for me.

"Yes. Just keep pretending that everything's fine. Gain his trust," Ivy says.

———

She isn't wrong. Gaining Aurielo's trust is what I need to do. Pretend that I'm okay with what I saw. That's an entirely different scenario that I'm struggling with.

I've finished work. Francesco picks me up at the usual time. I have no idea if he's still waiting in the lobby or if he's on a schedule and coming by when it's time for my shift to end.

I haven't been out to lunch since marrying Aurielo and being forced to have a bodyguard. But after what happened with the Bianchi family, I'm a little relieved someone cares enough to keep watch over me.

Aurielo wants to protect me.

At least that's what I tell myself.

I hate to think that the whole reason Francesco is still shuttling me to work, following me around, keeping an eye on me is that he doesn't trust me.

Shuffling out of my shoes the minute I'm inside the front door, I glance over my shoulder at Francesco. "Where's Ashton?" I don't know if he's been sequestered to his room like I was yesterday or if he's somewhere else in the house.

Francesco raises an eyebrow. "How would I know? Go upstairs."

I press my lips together.

Fighting isn't going to help me gain anyone's trust.

"Okay," I say and do as he instructs. I head up the stairwell. Hopefully, he won't force me to my bedroom. I want to see my son and find out how his day was at school.

Francesco doesn't stop me when I reach Ashton's room and open the door.

"Mommy!" Ashton grins. His eyes are bright and wide. He drops his pencil at his new desk that's been delivered to his bedroom and rushes over to me for a hug.

Aurielo sits at the edge of the windowsill and sits up straighter when I enter.

"Hey, Ash. How was school?" I ask, embracing him in a tight hug.

"Hard," Ashton says. He scrunches his nose. "They're making us do math. It's so confusing."

I ruffle his hair and kiss his cheek.

"Mom," he whines and wipes away my kiss.

I laugh under my breath and roll my eyes. Five, and he's already acting like a teenager. Is this what I get to look forward to when he gets older?

"How was work?" Aurielo asks, pushing himself off the windowsill as he stands, arms folded across his chest.

His posture is defensive.

"Better than yesterday," I say.

I realize I didn't tell him about Cora and losing her. Now isn't the time, with Ashton in the room. While he knows that I'm a nurse, I try to shield him from the grief and emotional difficulties of my job.

Aurielo's brow furrows, but he doesn't say anything.

"Were you helping him with his schoolwork?" I ask.

"He was checking my answers. But he won't give me the right ones," Ashton whines.

Aurielo glances down at Ashton. "You won't learn if you can't do it on your own. I won't be in class with you tomorrow to feed you the answers."

"You're mean," Ashton says. He squeezes me tighter in his embrace.

Aurielo is mean. Not because of how he's trying to teach Ashton, but because of the other things that he's done. The atrocities that Ashton is too young to understand.

"How about I help you with your homework?" I suggest. "Maybe we can try to figure out how to come to the answer together."

He untangles from my embrace and takes my hand, leading me to his new desk. Did Aurielo order that for him?

I bend down, and he shows me his math problems. It's a multiplication table.

He was doing addition and subtraction at his previous school, and it seems his grasp of multiplication is different from addition based on every answer on his sheet of paper.

"Have you looked these over yet?" I ask, glancing up at Aurielo.

"Twice," he says.

————

After spending the next hour helping Ashton learn multiplication and then double-checking the answers that he came up with again, he puts away his homework.

Aurielo has already vanished out of the bedroom. I'm not sure if he's busy interrogating a suspect, making us dinner, or doing some other mobster task that I'm not to know about.

"Do you want to go downstairs and head outside for a bit?" I ask Ashton.

He's going to say yes.

The garden is the perfect excuse for me to see how much trouble we'll get into for wandering around the house again.

No one said we had to stay in the bedroom for the rest of the day. If I avoid the basement, I assume I'll be okay.

That had to be why Alessandro, yesterday, whisked us upstairs.

Quietly, I open the bedroom door. I don't need to call attention to us heading out of the room and outside.

Ashton doesn't seem to have the same idea.

He isn't the least bit quiet, and I don't have the heart to tell him to keep quiet. I don't want him to fear Aurielo or the men here.

"Mommy," Ashton says. "Can we play catch like I did the other day?"

My heart aches at his question. "I don't have a ball, but maybe we can find one in the garden."

I doubt there's one just lying around, but I will ask Aurielo later if he can order one and have it delivered to the house for Ashton.

We head down the stairs and through the foyer to the hallway.

"Off to the garden?" Aurielo asks, coming around the darkened corner.

My mouth is dry. I don't want to be nervous, but I am while in his presence. I need to make him believe that I trust him. That's no easy feat.

"Yes," I say.

"Will you play catch with me?" Ashton asks him.

My heart aches at Ashton's question. I don't want him to bond with Aurielo. It will only make it harder for us to leave.

"Sure, buddy. But then I have to help make dinner for you and your mom."

Aurielo leads us to the garden and opens the door, gesturing for us to step outside.

"I'll be right back," he says and shuts the door.

A minute later, he's returned with a ball and pitcher's glove.

They head out to the center of the courtyard. The ground is a lush, soft grass, and I take a seat, watching the two of them interact.

"Hey, what happened to the swing?" I ask, remembering its appearance from the last time that I came out here and was surprised to find it in ruins.

"We got into a fight. The swing won," Aurielo mutters.

Okay.

Maybe it's better if I don't know about his violent tendencies. I saw enough for a lifetime last night.

It's why I need to take Ashton far away from here.

———

After dinner and putting Ashton to bed, I'm reluctant to find my way into our bedroom. I don't know what Aurielo will expect from me.

Ivy told me to play nice, make him believe I trust him, but does that mean giving myself over to him again?

The sex a few nights ago was phenomenal, but after what I witnessed last night, my desire has disappeared.

I'm afraid of Aurielo. While he hasn't hurt me yet, I can't help but worry and wonder. If I don't do what he asks, will he turn on me?

Could I find myself in prison?

I'm not safe. I'll never be safe until I'm free.

I grab my pajamas and head into the bathroom to shower. I keep hearing my sister's words over in my head that I need to make it convincing that I trust him.

But I don't trust Aurielo.

And I'm horrible at being deceitful. I don't have it in me to be someone I'm not. But I want to survive and get away and do what's best for my son.

I have to play the part.

Finishing my shower, I shut the water off, dry off with a towel, and dress.

The minute I'm out of the bathroom, Aurielo is practically on me.

"We need to talk."

This has to be about what I saw last night. He wanted to talk last night, too. I avoided him as best I could, but I don't think he's going to let me keep avoiding the situation.

"I know," I say and skirt past him for the bed. I climb under the covers and reach for the book that he loaned me.

I need a distraction.

Although I doubt I'll be able to concentrate on a single page with his intense stare on me.

"Do you?" he asks, pinning me with his gaze.

"I shouldn't have gone wandering around the house," I say.

He snorts under his breath. "Tell me about it. Snooping is more like it," he mutters.

"I'm sorry. I won't do it again."

It's the truth. I have no intention of sneaking back down into the basement. I don't want to witness the horrors of what men like Aurielo are capable of doing to other men.

"You're damned right you won't," he snaps. His eyes tighten, and he strips off his shirt.

I should glance away.

But I can't.

He stalks to the dresser and grabs a fresh change of boxers. He strips down completely naked. He's not the least bit modest or uncomfortable undressing in front of me.

I wish I could be quite so bold.

It's hard not to let my gaze linger as I stare at his naked form. His chest muscles are taut. I want to reach out and run my fingers down his torso, but I keep my hands gripped tight to the book. The book that I don't have the least bit of interest in reading tonight.

He doesn't bother putting on the clean boxers as I thought.

No.

Instead, he stalks toward me, naked.

My breath catches in my throat.

Does he realize the effect he has on me? The room feels warm. Hot, in fact.

I push the covers down to my lap. I'm propped up with two pillows so I can read, but my focus is entirely on Aurielo's naked form.

"I can't protect you if you go wandering into places that you don't belong," Aurielo scolds.

He's not wrong.

"I won't do it again." I have no desire to see his fist slamming into another man's body. I shiver involuntarily, remembering the scene.

"What's going through your head, *Micetta*?" Aurielo asks. He stops just beside the bed, his boxers in his hand. I hadn't even realized he'd been holding the thin piece of fabric, but he's made no intention of wearing the clothes.

"You're naked." The words squeak out.

"I hadn't noticed." He smirks and glances me over. "You look flushed, Karina. Are you feeling all right?"

He's playing with me. He must be. Of course, he knows that the reaction he sees is because of what he's doing. It's not every day I see a gorgeous, naked man at my bedside.

I swallow nervously. "I'm fine. You should put something on before you get cold."

"Is that what you really want?" Aurielo asks.

"Yes," I rasp. I don't sound the least bit convincing.

He shrugs and pulls on his boxers, doing as I've asked of him. I can't help but feel disappointed, but it's for the best. We can't be sleeping together, aside from actually sleeping.

"That's too bad. I was hoping to give you a full body massage," Aurielo says as he shuffles around the bed and climbs under the covers.

My cheeks must be burning. I'm sweltering under the covers. Did he turn the heat up in the bedroom to make me want to strip down naked and join him?

I don't see a separate thermostat for his bedroom, but I wouldn't put anything past him.

I groan and roll from my back onto my side, facing away from him. I toss the book on the bedside table. There's no way I'm going to get two words read at this rate. The only thing I can still see is Aurielo's naked torso in my head.

Fuck.

I've never felt so horny in my life. Not even during my pregnancy when I was craving sex. My vibrator had to suffice at the time. But I don't have that now, and if I so much as touch myself, Aurielo might find out.

The temptation is there, the curiosity of how he'd react, but I'm nervous too. He's hot and domineering. I'm not sure how he'd react to his wife masturbating in bed beside him.

I'm sure he has plenty of fantasies, and he probably does something about it in the shower, where no one else has to know.

"Goodnight," Aurielo says and reaches across me to turn off the light.

I can smell him.

It's a mix of wood and sweat. His scent is intoxicating.

I inhale a sharp breath.

Aurielo stares down at me.

Caught.

"Everything okay, *Micetta*?" he asks. There's a smile on his lips, like he knows what I just did.

Fuck my life.

Seriously, could my night get any worse?

"Goodnight," I mutter and roll onto my stomach, burying my face in the pillow.

He chuckles beside me. His mood is light. I don't understand how, after all he's seen and done, he can be so chipper and warm. It doesn't fit.

He doesn't fit the mold that I've seen and expected. It bothers me.

I should hate him.

Despise him. And not be the least bit aroused by him.

But my body wants him. Hell, *I* want him.

Who am I to say no?

But it's too dangerous. There's too much at stake, not including my son.

The darkness is a welcome distraction, but I can still smell him on the sheets and all around me. He rolls around, the bed shifting as Aurielo tries to make himself comfortable.

"You smell like fucking Christmas," he mutters grumpily against the pillows as he shuffles around on the mattress.

"Thanks?" I don't know what to make of his comment.

How the hell do I smell like Christmas?

I used whatever shampoo and conditioner were in the bathroom. However, it wasn't the same stuff that he used. He's probably just not used to the scent.

I roll onto my side.

His eyes are wide open, and I inhale a sharp breath. I didn't expect his intense gaze to stare back at me.

I want to roll around, pretend I didn't notice his glare in the darkness, but I can't look away. It's like a staring contest now where whoever glances away first loses.

And I never lose.

## 31

## AURIELO

The heat of the bedroom sizzles. I'm barely wearing anything, a flimsy pair of boxers, and I want to strip off the covers.

How the hell is Karina still wearing her pajamas in bed?

Although the covers are pushed down at her waist.

I thought she was asleep until she rolled over and caught me staring at her. Now she doesn't look away.

I'm caught between pretending to be asleep with my eyes open, which sounds even more ridiculous in my head, or waiting for her to submit and give in, letting me win.

A Rinaldi never backs down from a challenge.

I get a whiff of her scent from showering. She smells like cinnamon and spice. I want to lean in and brush my lips against hers. But I can't do that.

Somewhere in my stupid state of mind, I tell her she smells like Christmas, and her response is clear that she can't tell it's a compliment. I should have kept my mouth shut.

Which is what I'm doing now, staring at her.

And she's staring back.

I don't do well when I'm tired, and I'm feeling cranky.

My mind is racing, but nothing I say will take back what she saw last night. I can't change who I am or what I do. She knew that when she agreed to marry me.

Well, it was life or death.

She finally blinks and shuts her eyes. I win. Although I don't feel any better. Not even in the slightest.

"Goodnight," I whisper.

"Why?"

"Why what?" I ask.

Her eyes flash open.

"Why bring him to the house?"

It takes me a second to piece together what she's asking. "The man from last night whom you saw in the basement? It's where we keep our prisoners, *Micetta*. We can't go interrogating men in hotel rooms."

"Worried you'll have to marry a second wife if someone stumbles into the room."

Ouch.

"No, you're the only one for me." I reach for her jaw, keeping her gaze on me. "I take my vows of marriage very seriously."

It's not something we've spoken about, but being married to Karina, I don't intend to let another man touch my wife.

I also won't break my vows.

We're married. It's as simple as that.

"But you don't love me," Karina whispers. Her eyes have darkened a deeper, richer hue, like the ocean.

"And that upsets you?" She can't believe after a few days that I've fallen madly in love with her.

She shakes her head no. "I don't understand how you can marry me and not want someone who makes you feel whole."

Is that what she thinks of marriage? That it will complete her. That's a storybook ending.

Love like that isn't real.

I don't believe in fantasies or fairytales.

We make our destiny, and mine involved saving Karina's life. I don't regret my choices. Not even for a moment.

"My parents had an arranged marriage," I whisper, staring at her as I pull my hand back and rest it beneath the pillow. "They grew to care for one another, and more importantly, he protected her."

"Is that why you saved me?" Karina asks. "Because you're a great big protector?"

I laugh at her remark and roll onto my back. "Honestly, I've never thought of myself like that. Being an interrogator for Alessandro, I don't usually protect anyone except the secrets our family keeps."

"And what secrets might those be?"

"Nice try." She's not getting anything juicy out of me. The secrets I keep will go with me to my grave.

———

It's late by the time I fall asleep and morning roars its ugly head far before I'd like to wake up.

The alarm for Karina to wake blares, and I slam the damn thing off while she fumbles out of bed.

I don't bother trying to go back to sleep. I sit up in bed, prop myself up with the extra pillows, the blanket at my waist, while I watch her meander around in the bedroom.

Karina grabs her clothes from the dresser and heads for the bathroom, shutting the door behind herself.

Just once, I'd like a show.

A striptease.

Anything to satisfy my aching desire that she's stirred, especially this morning.

Will I ever get to see her naked again and trembling in my arms? Maybe if I play my cards right, but she's been hesitant since the encounter in the basement.

I run my fingers through my hair. It was never my intention for her to witness what I do for a living. While it may not be a secret, knowing and seeing are two different things entirely.

I've scared her.

She probably thinks of me as a savage beast, an animal that enjoys torturing and humiliating scum-sucking low lives.

I don't enjoy the work, but it pays handsomely, and I like my lavish lifestyle. Besides, working for Alessandro has its perks. I'd never have married Karina if I wasn't an interrogator.

We probably wouldn't have met again, either.

The bathroom door squeaks open, and Karina steps out in jeans and a t-shirt. "You wear that to work?" I ask.

She looks sexy. I want to rip the clothes she just put on right off her.

"Yes, I change into my scrubs when I get on the unit," Karina says. Her brow knits. "You're only now noticing that I don't wear my work clothes to work?"

I haven't been observant lately. At least not in terms of what she wears. It's not like I keep track of her outfits or wardrobe. I've been preoccupied with other matters.

"Give me a break, it's early, and I'm exhausted." It's the truth.

She heads to the dresser, retrieves a pair of socks, and sits on the edge of the bed while she puts them on. "Can we go to the park as a family? Play ball? Do normal family things and maybe have dinner out?" Karina asks while she slips her socks on.

She's asking a lot, but I don't see the harm. If this is her olive branch, I'll take it.

"I don't see why not." I'll have to make sure Francesco isn't busy, or another bodyguard can accompany us if we're going off the compound. "How about I pick you up after work and bring

Ashton? He should be done with school about the same time."

## 32

## KARINA

The plan is in motion.

I've already notified Ivy. Aurielo hasn't told me what park he's planning on taking me to, but there's one close to the hospital. I intend to suggest we head there, let him and Ashton play catch for a bit before Ivy causes a distraction.

Hopefully, it works.

My stomach has been in knots all afternoon.

The day ticks by slowly, and if all goes according to plan, I'll be out of the city tonight.

No one will know what happened to Ashton or me.

Except for Ivy.

And even she won't know where we're going. It's for her own safety. The less she knows, the better.

She's dropping off her car near the park and grabbing a rental car to plow into the park's fire hydrant.

I just hope it works, and I can get Aurielo away from Ashton long enough to run.

"How was work?" Aurielo asks, offering a friendly smile as I see the three of them hanging out in the lobby of the hospital.

"Busy." It's the truth.

I still haven't told him about the other day, when a patient died. It's not that we don't have kids die on the unit, but Cora, she'd been around so long that I really didn't think she'd go. At least not so soon.

"Ready for a little fun?" Aurielo asks. Somehow I think the question is more for Ashton than for me.

Francesco grunts under his breath. He doesn't look the least bit amused about this family outing. As always, he dresses sharply. Today is no different. He'll stand out at the park, but there's not much that I can do about that small fact.

Aurielo at least thought to wear jeans and a white dress shirt. He looks undeniably hot.

Ashton clutches Aurielo's hand until he sees me and runs right for me, throwing his arms around me as I bend down to embrace him with a tight squeeze.

"Mommy!"

"How's my favorite little man?" I ask. It feels wonderful to know that he's safe in my arms.

That's why I have to do this.

Protect him.

At all costs.

"We get to play ball at the park!" Ashton squeals as he clutches my hand.

Together, we wander outside of the hospital, and I lead the way, heading toward the park. Aurielo and Francesco follow without much fuss. My hands are sweaty from nervousness.

Ivy's car is parked on one side of the park, a fire hydrant sits at the opposite end.

Perfect.

I let go of Ashton's hand after we cross the street, letting him run along the grass into the park.

"You sure that's a good idea?" Aurielo stalks up beside me.

"What?"

"Letting him run off ahead of you like that. Someone could snatch him."

Yeah, me.

I press my lips tight and shoot a glance at him. "You have your bodyguard here. We'll be fine. It's still plenty light out, and the boy needs outside time to run around and have fun. Did you bring your ball and glove?" I ask.

Aurielo reveals a backpack that I hadn't noticed earlier swung on his opposite shoulder. "I did," he says.

"Good. I'm sure Ashton will be excited to play ball with you at the park." I fold my arms across my chest. The slight breeze is cool this afternoon but feels good, sending goosebumps along my arms.

My stomach is a coil of knots as I keep my gaze on both Ashton and the nearby fire hydrant. I hope the plan works and that Aurielo and Francesco pull their attention from Ashton long enough for me to grab him and lure him to the car unnoticed.

A lot is playing on the distraction.

Aurielo drops his backpack and kneels down, one knee on the ground while he unzips the black bag and retrieves a baseball and two gloves. This time, he has one for Ashton.

I'm a shitty mother, taking my son away from his father.

But that father is a mobster.

What other choice do I have?

I didn't know the man I slept with killed and tortured people for a living. I have to do what's best for my child, and pulling him out of a tough situation, no matter how good it looks and appears on the outside, is important.

This new life is superficial.

The private school Ashton is enrolled in, his father wanting to play ball with him, the mansion we live in, it's all fake.

It has to be, or else I'm making the biggest mistake of my life.

No.

My stomach churns. I shove my hands into my pockets, hoping that no one notices the slight tremble. Nervous is the biggest understatement.

I'm trying not to be obvious by staring at the fire hydrant.

Ivy gave me the time that she would create the distraction, but that assumed traffic was perfectly timed. And it's the city. Traffic sucks.

Also, I don't know the make or model of the rental car that she grabbed last minute. So, I'll be as surprised by the accident as Aurielo and Francesco.

I just have to act on instinct.

Not react.

Aurielo hurries over to Ashton and bends down, handing him a glove. They exchange a few words and then a hug.

I'm going to be sick.

I'm doing this for Ashton.

He deserves safety. Protection. Love.

Aurielo can't give him all those things. Maybe one. I'm not even sure which.

They toss the ball back and forth. Time feels as though it stretches on forever.

I inch closer to Ashton. I need to be ready.

Tires squeal.

Now's my chance.

A bright red SUV plows across the grass, onto the sidewalk and then slams into the fire hydrant.

I grab Ashton and hightail it for Ivy's parked car. It's not far from us, and we have the advantage. Aurielo is several feet in the opposite direction.

The car smashing the fire hydrant stole his attention.

I can't turn around and see if Aurielo or Francesco noticed us flee and followed us. If I do, it'll slow us down.

I hurry to the car. The doors are left open, and I practically shove Ashton into the backseat.

"Buckle up!" I order and hurry to the driver's side, open the door, and leap into the vehicle. I lock the doors, grab the keys from the visor, and start the engine.

Fuck.

I glance out the window, and Aurielo is almost at the door. He's gaining on us, and he looks pissed.

I put the car in drive and slam on the gas—I thunderbolt out into traffic.

Vehicles honk at me for cutting them off as I veer into the lane and hurry, rushing away from the park. I can't let Aurielo catch up with us.

———

"Mommy," Ashton is whining in the backseat.

How do I explain what the hell just happened?

"It's okay, buddy. Are you buckled into your booster seat?" I hate that I didn't have time to secure the seat. I have to trust that Ivy had it ready, and Ashton latched the buckle himself.

Every so often, I glance back in the rearview mirror.

I head for the back roads to exit the city. If I take the highway, there could be others after me, and they know the vehicle that I'm driving. It wouldn't be hard to spot us.

Will Aurielo call for reinforcements?

Another glance in the mirror. Just a bunch of traffic. No one is suspicious. Francesco hasn't tailed us yet.

That's good news.

I head away from the hospital. Francesco and Aurielo would have had to return to the hospital to get the car.

My stomach is churning as I grip the steering wheel.

Ivy.

What was her plan? She told me not to worry. She'd have it handled, but what did she plan to do after she hit the fire hydrant?

Did she drive away?

Did Francesco or Aurielo capture her?

My bottom lip trembles at the horrible notion that Ivy could be interrogated by Aurielo.

No.

He wouldn't torture my sister. Would he?

# 33

## AURIELO

What the fuck just happened?

Francesco runs toward the vehicle that just plowed into the fire hydrant, spraying water everywhere.

It caught me off-guard.

So did Karina.

After the initial stun of the car accident, I spin around to make sure Ashton is all right, and Karina is rushing him across the lawn into a waiting vehicle.

Shit.

She played me.

"Aurielo!" Francesco shouts for me.

I can't deal with whatever it is he needs right now. Call 9-1-1 if the driver needs medical assistance.

I chase after the vehicle, and just as I get close enough to grab for the door handle, she bolts into traffic, nearly causing a four-car collision to get away.

I swear if she hurts a hair on my son's head, she'll pay.

"Aurielo!" Francesco calls for me again. His voice is distant, and I grumble and hustle to the opposite side to see what the hell the commotion is all about.

Fuck it.

Ivy Cole. Karina's twin sister.

"I'll get the car," Francesco says as he jets out across traffic, running a couple of blocks toward the hospital's parking lot. He's on the same page as me.

"You did this on purpose," I snarl as I rush toward the red SUV.

Ivy is slumped forward. Her head must have hit the steering wheel or the window. There's a gash across her forehead and blood along her hairline.

Her eyelids flutter open at the sound of my voice. She smiles as blood drips down her cheek. "You'll never find her."

———

"I won't tell you anything," Ivy says.

We hauled her ass out of the vehicle and into our car, taking her with us back to the compound for interrogation.

Forced into a chair in the prison basement, her bare feet slide against the cold cement floor.

"You can't keep me in here forever."

She is so much like her sister.

Which one of them is older?

It doesn't matter. My interrogation isn't about her.

"Where did your sister take my son?" I seethe, standing over her.

Ivy's hands are tied behind her back, bound with rope. I cleaned up the gash on her forehead with a damp rag and alcohol to let her feel a dash of pain.

"I don't know what you're talking about," Ivy says.

"Are you really going to pretend today was a coincidence?" I ask, huffing under my breath. "You can't be that stupid, Ivy. You know what I do for a living. I'm sure Karina already told you."

"Yes! She told me that you're a monster, and now I get to see it firsthand." Her eyes glint.

There's a fierce determination behind her gaze.

"Did she happen to mention how I saved her life?" I pull up a stool and pin her with my stare. "I'll bet she forgot to mention that part, how Don Rinaldi wanted me to execute her, and I saved her life."

"You're a liar," Ivy says.

It's just the two of us alone in the prison cell. When I want to be released from behind the iron bars, I'll shout out to Giovan to let me out. It prevents carrying a key inside the holding cell and an inmate from escaping.

"Why would I lie to you?" I ask.

"You want to see your son."

She isn't wrong, but I'm not lying. "I do want to see Ashton. He is my son, like you said, my flesh and blood. But I don't want to hurt him or Karina."

Her eyes tighten. "You're a monster. You kidnapped my sister, forced her to marry you, and probably raped her."

I'm appalled. I stand, the stool squeaking as I push it away. "Is that what you think? Is that what she said?"

I can't believe her. I never forced myself physically on Karina, ever. I've also been a firm believer in consent. I don't get my jollies off on a woman being afraid or not interested. There are plenty of women throwing themselves at me. I don't need to be that monster.

"She didn't have to," Ivy says. "Just look at you. Your hands were all over me at the apartment. That wasn't consensual!"

I exhale a heavy sigh and pinch the bridge of my nose. "I warned your sister that I would search her after she went into the apartment if she was leaving me outside in the hallway."

She snorts. "I don't believe you."

I shrug. "Don't care. I'm telling the truth. You don't know anything about my relationship with Karina." Does she know that we had sex this week? I'd guess not. Ivy hasn't brought it up.

"I know enough. She wanted to get away from you."

Ivy is right. Karina doesn't trust me. It's because of what she saw me do to that man in the prison. I run a hand through my hair, growling.

"Fuck!" I kick the stool that I sat on moments earlier across the prison cell, the wood slamming into the metal bars.

If I so much as lay a finger on Ivy, it'll prove to Karina that I'm the savage she believes me to be.

Giovan hurries down the stairs, checking on me. I didn't call him down, but I wasn't particularly quiet with the stupid wood stool, either. The damned thing is now broken, one of the legs knocked off. I toss the broken leg through the iron slat, outside the prison doors.

The last thing I need is Ivy attempting to grab it as a weapon, although she is still tied up. But I don't take my gaze off her.

"Tell me where my family is."

Ivy shrugs. "Upstairs?"

I stalk closer, brooding over her. "I'll bet you think you're funny."

"I'm a riot at parties," Ivy quips.

She looks so much like Karina. The resemblance makes my stomach knot. If it were Karina, I would want to tear off her clothes and fuck her in the prison cell.

It's deceptive for her to look so much like her sister, my wife.

"I'll bet you are," I mutter under my breath. "I need to talk to Karina. How have you been communicating with her? At work?"

I took her cell phone the minute she came with me and agreed to marry me for protection.

"Yeah, sure."

I'm not convinced.

I reach into her handbag that we snagged with us when she was grabbed at the park. I had hoped there'd been some inclination of where Karina had taken Ashton, but it had been just her phone, wallet, and a stick of gum.

I retrieve her phone.

"Passcode?" I ask.

She shakes her head.

"Lucky me. It uses your finger." I bring the phone around from behind her chair and force her to touch the fingerprint pad to unlock her phone. "You should be thanking me. Anyone else and I'd have cut off their finger."

Ivy snarls at my remark. "See! That's why she ran."

I roll my eyes. "Quit being so dramatic. I'm not going to hurt my son or my wife," I say.

Why can't she believe me?

I glance through her messages. There aren't any texts.

That's odd.

She must have deleted them before the accident. It's obvious Karina and Ivy planned the getaway.

I flip through the contacts and then previous numbers. There's one that called her several times. "Who is this?" I ask.

"My therapist," Ivy says.

I hit call and wait for the other person to answer the phone.

"Ivy? Are you okay?" Karina asks, her voice out of breath.

"No, she's not," I say. "You have my son. Bring him back to the compound, or I kill your sister."

"Don't listen to him!" Ivy screams.

I hang up the phone and open a tracking app that Ivy previously installed. Apparently, they were sharing each other's location. I don't know whether it was on purpose or not, but Karina is at the bus station. At least her phone is, and given the fact I just spoke with her, she should be too.

## 34

### KARINA

Standing outside, I clutch Ashton's hand in mine, keeping him close against me. It's hard not to feel paranoid.

Aurielo is out there, hunting me down.

We have only the clothes on our backs.

I bought two bus tickets and plan on changing routes again, just to ensure that we can't be tracked.

I toss my phone into the garbage. I can't take any chances since Aurielo figured out the phone number belongs to me. If there is any chance that he can track me, I have to be careful and be two steps ahead of him.

While we're waiting for the bus, Aurielo breezes in like nothing happened.

"Hey, Ashton!" Aurielo's eyes are cold, but the smile on his face makes Ash fall right into his trap, hook, line, and sinker.

Shit.

"Aurielo!" Ashton squeals and runs to him.

It's taken no time for the two of them to bond.

I should have been more careful and kept Ashton away. But I did try to hide him from Aurielo.

What more could I do?

"How about we head home?" Aurielo asks, ruffling Ash's hair after a firm hug. He keeps an arm wrapped around my son.

I get a glimpse of his gun in his holster.

My mouth is dry.

I feel threatened. I'm sure that's the point.

"Come on, Mommy," Ashton says, waiting for me to join them.

Reluctantly, I sigh and trudge behind, joining Aurielo back at his car. At least Francesco isn't driving. I take a little relief in not having to face him, too.

"Backseat, kiddo," Aurielo orders. He opens the car door.

At least there's a booster seat for my son.

Ashton climbs into the booster and secures his seatbelt.

"You have your own car," Aurielo says and slams the backdoor shut.

"What?" I scoff. He isn't really taking my son from me. Is he?

His gazes tightens, and he folds his arms across his chest. "If you want to see your son, you'll meet me at home. Do you need the address?" Aurielo asks.

I can't abandon Ashton. "Let me ride with you." We can worry about the car later.

"That's not a good idea. I don't trust you," Aurielo says. He glances me over.

What does he think I'm going to do?

"Please, Aurielo, let me be with my son."

He humphs under his breath. "And you can, as soon as you return home."

"Is Ivy—" I'm afraid to finish my thought.

Dead.

I need to know the truth. Maybe I can fight Aurielo and grab Ashton, make a break for it.

How far would we get?

Aurielo will come looking for us. He won't ever give up, especially now that he knows Ashton is his son.

"Yes," Aurielo says as he unfolds his arms and digs the keys out of his pocket. He hits the auto start on the car, setting the engine roaring to life.

My bottom lip trembles. The words don't come. I want to tell him he's a ruthless monster. That I will never love him and am staying with him is out of fear and necessity, not desire.

"Yes, Ivy is back at the house," Aurielo says, finishing his sentence.

A sob slips past my lips, and I cover my mouth.

Is she alive?

He only said that she was back at the house. That doesn't mean she's alive. It also doesn't mean that she's dead.

The world around me seems to spin, and I pinch the bridge of my nose. The tears don't stop leaking, no matter how hard I wish them away. If only I could redo this week, go back in time, stop myself from entering that stupid hotel room.

But I can't.

This is my life.

For better or worse. Until death do us part.

———

There's little choice. I follow Aurielo back to the mansion.

He lets me follow him, waits until I get into my car and am tailing him before he heads for the highway.

My fingers grip the steering wheel as though my life depends on it.

Maybe it does.

My son is in the vehicle in front of me. I want to rescue Ashton, but I won't let him get hurt. I keep a safe distance, ensuring that I won't crash the vehicle, although the thought crosses my mind: *Slam into his SUV. Snag my son. Run.*

We already tried one version of that earlier this afternoon, and it didn't go over well.

Arriving back at the mansion, I pull up out front, and there's a guard standing with a semi-automatic weapon slung over his shoulder.

Shit.

Is that intended to scare me?

It's working.

"Mommy!" Ashton squeals as he jumps out of the backseat and rushes toward me.

I embrace him in one of the biggest hugs, memorizing every detail, including how he feels in my arms. I don't ever want to let go.

But Ashton shimmies out of my grasp. "Mom," he whines.

Reluctantly, I let go. What other choice do I have?

"Inside," Aurielo commands as he stomps up the steps and in through the front door.

I clasp Ashton's hand and lead him inside. Exhaling a heavy breath, I can't help but worry if I'll ever see daylight again.

Will Aurielo or his men force me into the prison basement?

"Upstairs," Aurielo shoots off another order.

I breathe a sigh of relief and head up the stairs. Aurielo is right on my heel, barely giving me any space or room to waltz up the steps.

Ashton is practically attached to my hip as we approach his bedroom. There's already a guard standing outside the door.

They couldn't bother to wait until we came home.

Weird.

Turning the handle, I open Ashton's bedroom door, and he rushes past me.

Ivy is sitting at the edge of the bed, her hands in her lap. She jumps at the sound of the door.

"Ivy?" I hurry across the room and throw my arms around her as she stands. She looks better than I feel. My stomach is tumbling in somersaults. My hands won't stop shaking, and I pull her tight for a hug. "You're okay."

Relief floods through me.

"Yeah, no thanks to him," Ivy mutters, glancing up at Aurielo in the door jamb.

I release my hold around my sister and spin around on my heels. "What the hell did you do to her?"

"Nothing she didn't already deserve," Aurielo says. He nods toward Ivy. "Nice to see you up."

"What does that mean?" I ask. What is Aurielo talking about?

"Probably because I was tied to a chair in prison downstairs and interrogated!" Ivy points at Aurielo. "You're a monster."

"You plotted to have my son kidnapped!" Aurielo snaps. His nostrils flare, and his gaze tightens before he turns and slams the bedroom shut.

# 35

## AURIELO

Harsh. There's no other way to be around Karina. She deserves what she gets. Taking my son away from me, stealing him, running away to go where, exactly?

Karina clearly isn't much of a planner. She flies by the seat of her pants. Or maybe her panties.

I doubt Karina came up with the plan. Ivy must have been behind it. She definitely seems the type.

I allowed Giovan to release Ivy out of prison and to Ashton's bedroom. Giovan can grab a cot and let the two of them share a room for a while.

Trusting Ivy not to go to the cops isn't an option. We don't normally catch and release.

When we get hold of a prisoner, we torture and kill.

But Ivy looks exactly like Karina, and laying a finger on her feels wrong.

Besides, Karina would never forgive me if I hurt her sister. I saw the way that Karina looked at me after she witnessed a glimpse of an interrogation.

I instruct Giovan to bring up dinner to Ivy, Ashton, and Karina. I can't deal with them. Not right now. I need to unwind, cool off, and expel some energy.

Not an easy task, given my mood.

I head down the stairs to the private gym with workout gear. I wrap my hands and slip on a set of gloves before pounding the shit out of the pole bag.

It feels good, but there's no opponent. I want to duck and dodge blows, but I'll take what I can get tonight.

After an hour of beating the shit out of the bag, I remove the gloves and head up to the bedroom for a shower.

The cold water burns against my skin. My heart is still racing, but it doesn't dull the ache in my stomach or my chest.

Karina is trouble.

The way she makes me feel, all knotted up inside, I don't like it.

I'm usually better at controlling how I feel, but she's making me crazy. Just knowing that she's across the hall makes me rock hard.

Fuck.

I don't want to think about her. And I certainly don't want to stroke myself thinking about her.

Anger sizzles beneath my veins, but it doesn't stop my body from having a mind of its own.

I force the water colder.

I need to chill the hell out.

———

It's late. I can't avoid Karina forever. Giovan was supposed to bring a cot up to Ashton's room for Ivy to sleep on.

But Karina is joining me in our bedroom.

Whether she wants to or not, she's mine, and I intend to keep a close eye on her.

I don't bother with a shirt, but I slip on a pair of blue jeans. My feet are bare. I patter across the hallway, past Giovan.

He's standing guard.

"It's been quiet for a while," he says.

"Good."

Hopefully, they're not concocting another scenario. At least we have close eyes on them. I wouldn't put it past Alessandro to suggest installing a security camera in the room.

He hasn't yet, though, or else I'm sure I'd know about it.

I don't bother knocking. I yank the door open and trudge inside. I'm not quiet, but I don't announce my presence, either.

Ashton is asleep in bed.

I'm relieved the kid can sleep after what transpired today.

I pin Karina with my stare. "Come with me." It's not a question. It's a command.

She sighs and stands, getting up from the edge of the bed. "Goodnight," she says to Ivy, giving her a quick hug and kiss goodnight.

Ivy plops down onto the cot. It already has a blanket and pillow, but she clearly hasn't used it yet.

I wait for Karina by the door and quietly shut it after we step out into the hallway. "Bedroom. Now!"

"You don't have to order me around," she huffs.

Karina heads across the hallway to our bedroom and opens the door.

"Don't I? It doesn't seem like you know what the hell you should be doing." I follow her inside and shut the door rather abruptly behind me.

She jumps from the sound.

Karina is a bit on edge. I can see it in her reflection, her eyes wide, her breathing increasing.

Is she scared of me?

I don't want to be a monster, not to her. But I can't help who I am or what I am, for that matter.

She tugs her bottom lip between her teeth. Her gaze falters down my chest to my dark blue jeans and then back up again.

"See something you like?" I doubt she's ogling me. It's probably my imagination. But I'm hopeful.

What hot-blooded straight male isn't hopeful that a pretty lady wants him?

Karina folds her arms across her chest. It's a defensive move. You learn body language when interrogating suspects. Not that she's a suspect to be interrogated, but it's hard to separate some facets of life.

"No," she whispers. A soft puff of air escapes her lips.

I step closer, invading her personal space. "I don't believe you."

Her top lip curls as she snarls at me, proving me wrong. "I want nothing to do with you or your stupid mafia."

"Fine," I say and hold my hands up. "Be that way. You can sleep on the couch."

"What? No!"

I shrug and strip out of my jeans. I leave my boxers on tonight. I've already showered and changed. She missed the show.

She's standing there awkwardly while I breeze past her and pull back the covers, making myself at home. It is, after all, my bed.

Karina purses her lips, staring at me.

"You're lucky I have a soft spot for my wife. Anyone else tried to steal my son, and they'd be dead."

She gulps. Her tongue darts out and swipes across her lips. Karina appears nervous.

Good. She ought to be uncomfortable. The girl brought me to my knees with dread, worried sick about my son.

"I'm sorry," her voice is soft, barely audible.

"Don't say things you don't mean." I fluff the pillow behind me.

Words mean nothing if there's no intention behind them.

Karina patters across the room to the dresser and retrieves a pair of pajamas. On her way to the bathroom, she glances over her shoulder at me. "I just want what's best for my son."

"We both do," I say. Doesn't she realize that? I'm fighting to protect him. "The Bianchis are still out there. You can't just wander off. They'll find you. Torture you. Kill you."

Her bottom lip trembles, and she hurries the rest of the way into the bathroom, slamming the door shut.

I hear the bathroom fan buzz before she starts the water in the shower.

Did I upset her?

Probably. But she needs to hear the truth. She needs to know what she's up against. It's not just me being overly protective and overbearing. I'm trying to keep her safe. I'm trying desperately to keep my son safe.

Karina doesn't make that easy for me.

I shut off the lights and wait for her to ease out of the bathroom before I fall asleep. I'm not the least bit tired, and I want to talk to her. It doesn't surprise me that she rushed out of the room at the first chance of a conversation.

I'm bitter.

I can't help it. She snatched my son!

I toss the covers off. The bedroom is stuffy. Maybe it's me.

Sitting up in bed, I stare at the bathroom door, waiting for her to emerge. The shower shuts off. Any minute, she'll be dried off and dressed. She's probably hoping I'm asleep.

She's dead wrong.

# 36

## KARINA

I don't have to be in the same room to feel the tension brewing between us. Mostly, that energy is radiating off Aurielo, and I can't say I'm surprised.

I didn't consider what would happen if we got caught.

How had he tracked Ashton and me down at the bus station?

Ivy hadn't known where we were heading. She couldn't have spilled our location. But he had found my number, probably through my sister's phone.

Damn.

Just when I thought we might manage to get away and be safe.

I stay in the shower until the water runs cold and I'm forced to shut off the tap—anything to avoid Aurielo.

By the time I sneak into the bedroom, Aurielo is still wide awake. I purse my lips, unsure of what to say. Nothing is going to fix what happened today.

He doesn't trust me. He's not wrong, either. I betrayed him.

I have half a mind to sleep on the couch, but it doesn't look comfortable. But being under Aurielo's scrutiny, that's even less desirable.

I shut off the bathroom light and stalk toward the bed, pulling back the covers.

I'm waiting for him to say something like 'we need to talk' or 'I will never trust you again.'

Maybe it's coming, and I'm just impatient. The tension is brewing, and the heat is agonizing. I don't like conflict, let alone fighting.

"Let the water run cold?" Aurielo asks.

I slink under the covers and adjust the pillow as I shuffle down the mattress to get comfortable. It's hard to feel the least bit comfortable with him staring at me.

"What's that?" I play it off like I don't know what he's talking about. I'm not an idiot. I just got out of the shower. But at least maybe I can keep him talking and the conversation about something other than what I did today and my betrayal.

"You took a while in the shower," Aurielo says.

I roll onto my side, staring at him. Maybe I should be afraid of Aurielo, but I'm not.

I'm worried about my son, the world he'll see, experience, and how he'll become under the leadership of the mafia.

His role models should be positive influences, or at least people who don't torture, interrogate, and murder men.

"I didn't notice," I say and pretend to dust lint off my shoulder. It's a distraction, a way not to stare at him anymore as he continues pinning me with his gaze.

It's uncomfortable.

I'm sure it's why he does it. Aurielo is a mastermind with interrogations. He's probably well-versed in manipulation tactics as well.

"What was your plan?" Aurielo asks. He doesn't avoid the topic at all. "Runaway with Ashton, and then what? It's obvious you love your job. Were you really going to give it up? Why? Because you don't want to be married to me?"

It's a punch to my gut.

"What you did to that man, I can't just forgive and forget," I say.

Doesn't he realize that I don't want my son to become like him?

"You knew who I was the day we met."

I shake my head. "Not the first time." Certainly not when we conceived Ashton. I didn't know anything about Aurielo.

His nostrils flare as he breathes. Aurielo exhales heavily through his nose. "I'm not talking about when we fucked at my cousin's engagement party."

"Yes, I knew you were a monster and that's why I kept my son from you. Ivy was going to take care of him and keep him away from this life," I say. He has to realize I was doing it to protect Ashton.

Aurielo folds his arms across his chest. His biceps are huge. I try not to stare at his muscles. It doesn't help that he's not wearing a shirt. "How long was that plan going to last? You not seeing your son?"

I hate that he's right, but I would have done anything to protect Ashton. Maybe I should have let Ivy snatch him and disappear today, while I took her place in the vehicle that crashed into the fire hydrant.

Although I don't know how that would have turned out, except we are twins. But Aurielo can see right through us.

At least I feel like he can. Maybe I'm making more out of what we have than what exists between us.

"I'd do anything to protect him," I whisper. It's the truth.

"In case you haven't figured it out, *Micetta*, so would I."

———

Every day is the same. I go to work, and when my shift is done, Francesco accompanies me back to the mansion. Ashton is waiting upstairs for me in his bedroom that he shares with Ivy.

I'm not sure whether I'm grateful Ivy is here or not. She hasn't blamed me, but I can see the resentment in her eyes. She misses home. Although our house apartment wasn't flashy or prestigious in any way, it was still home. It was ours.

This place is cold. It's impersonal. My bedroom doesn't feel the least bit like my own space. That doesn't bother me nearly as much as Ashton and Ivy sharing a room.

My sister shouldn't have to share with him.

Maybe Alessandro wouldn't offer additional accommodations for me separate from my son, but I blame that on the fact we were forced to wed. He probably enjoys locking us into a bedroom together, making us play house.

I haven't had too many interactions with Don Rinaldi. He seems a million times scarier than Aurielo.

Aurielo and I exchange pleasantries in the evening before bed. It's superficial. Nothing more than an act of acceptance.

I've accepted this as my life.

He's locked me up inside either Ashton's bedroom or my own. There's always a guard standing outside the hallway.

I have no freedom other than the hours that I'm at work. And that is hardly classified as freedom.

I give Ashton a hug goodbye before being whisked down the stairs and out the door for my job. I don't know when Ivy leaves if she's even allowed off the grounds.

We haven't talked about it, and I'm hesitant to ask. No doubt she's pissed to be mixed up in the arrangement and forced to live under Rinaldi's roof.

I'm silent in the back of the vehicle, Francesco chauffeuring me to work. However, he's still hanging out in the lobby all day. Yesterday, I snuck down during a break to see if I could plan an escape sometime and he was seated facing the elevator across the lobby.

One glance at me, and I hit the button, riding the elevator back up.

He's not a man I want to deal with. Francesco is scary, and knowing that he's in Alessandro's ear, I need to be careful.

"Busy day planned?" Jocelyn asks as I meet up with her to get dressed for my shift.

I frown, not understanding her question. "The usual. Work." I have no idea what she's asking.

There's a sparkle in her eye and a grin that she is desperately trying to hide.

"What do you know?" I ask. I can feel the giddiness radiating right off her. It's not my birthday, or anyone else's on the unit, as far as I'm aware.

She presses her lips together and shakes her head. Jocelyn is trying to frown but failing miserably. Her bottom lip juts out a little too much. "Nothing." She slams her locker shut and slings the lanyard with her badge on over her head.

"Girl, you cannot keep a secret. Spill it!" I'm waiting for the dirt, the juice, the 4-1-1. Whatever news she has, it must be hot. "Did someone get hitched?" I doubt it beats my surprise elopement.

Jocelyn laughs. "Only you are that spontaneous. Which is rather funny because I never took you for a spontaneous person." She muses over her words for a few seconds and then opens her mouth to spill the secret. "Your hubby is coming today."

"What?" She has obliviously lost her mind.

"He's on the schedule. The whiteboard outside in the nurses' station. You didn't notice?"

I just got in this morning, and his name was definitely not on there yesterday.

"Why is he coming to my work?" The question is more for me than Jocelyn. I don't expect her to know what the hell is going on. Although she already has more information than I have, and it's pissing me off.

Her brow tightens. "Are you two fighting? I thought you'd be glad he's coming by this afternoon."

"This afternoon," I repeat.

Occasionally, we have visitors, special guests who come in, like sports celebrities that bring jerseys to sign and spend time with the kids for an afternoon.

Aurielo isn't a celebrity. He's not anyone special. I mean, he's a mobster! What the hell is he doing coming here? How could they let him come into the unit without vetting him first?

Sweat drips from my brow.

"Are you okay?" Jocelyn asks. "I can grab you a bottle of water from the fridge. Don't faint on me, okay?"

"I'm fine." I'm not the least bit okay. "He just took me by surprise, coming to visit. Is he taking me to lunch?" I don't intend to sound so damned selfish, but I can't wrap my head around why he would show up on the unit for the kids. It must be to see me. But why speak with the dragon, my supervisor, and have it on the whiteboard?

"No," Jocelyn says, and wraps an arm around my shoulder. "He's bringing presents for the kids."

What?

I'm stunned.

"Are you sure?" I ask. Maybe it was a different gentleman, but it's not like Aurielo has a common first name.

"One hundred percent. He asked the dragon for a list of ages and any special requests. You wouldn't believe how many kids asked for a cell phone!"

It's hard not to laugh, the smile forcing its way to my lips. "That sounds like the kids," I laugh. But it still doesn't sound like Aurielo.

———

He may as well have dressed as Santa with the number of presents he lugs inside. He's got two giant red satchels filled with presents that are wrapped, just like Christmas.

"Does someone want to tell him Christmas is a few months away?" I whisper to Jocelyn.

She shakes her head, a smirk on her face. "If I can sit on Santa's lap, I'll be naughty."

I smack her arm. "That's my husband." And she had the same thought I did. Maybe it's the red satchels that he's lugging around, room to room, distributing presents to the kids that make him seem a bit like Santa.

He doesn't have the long white beard, the belly, or the outfit. But I'll give it to him. He does make the kids' faces light up.

Dragon insists that I escort Aurielo from room to room. He's not allowed with the kids alone, and I'm relieved that the hospital has a few rules they still abide by. Not that accepting presents from the mafia is illegal, it just has my stomach in turmoil.

As we round the corner after the first section of rooms, I grab his arm and drag him into the supply closet. I need somewhere to talk to him in private, and the breakroom is too far away.

"What are you doing?" Aurielo asks.

I laugh. Is he seriously asking me that question?

"What am I doing?" I scoff. "I should be asking you what you're doing?" My voice raises an octave.

"Giving presents to kids," Aurielo says. "I thought I might cheer them up. And show you that I'm not a bad guy."

I snap my fingers and point at him. "And there's the ulterior motive that I was waiting for from you."

Aurielo glances around the supply closet. "Planning on keeping me locked up in here, or can I finish gifting presents to kids with cancer?"

Shit.

Did he really just say that?

Make me into the bad guy.

I open the door and gesture for him to step out of the closet. He heads down the hallway. I clasp my hands together in front of me. I have no choice but to follow him and force a smile. If I could chew him out right now, I would.

His nice guy act is just that, an act. He can fool my colleagues and a floor of sick kids, but he can't fool me.

# 37

# AURIELO

"Are you ever going to see past the monster that you see lurking inside of me?" I ask. It's obvious that's all she sees when she looks at me, that I brutally attacked an unarmed man. Well, he was more than just unarmed. He was bound to the chair, unable to move.

No one said it had to be a fair fight.

We're the mafia.

Besides, I treated Ivy with the utmost kindness during an interrogation. But Karina doesn't see it like that.

I'm the savage. And she's the saint.

Well, let me tell you something, she's no saint. Trying to steal my son from me, rob me of my family. She's a wolf in sheep's clothing—the true monster.

"It's hard to do that with you locking me inside the house all the time!" Karina shouts.

The walls practically vibrate, and I'm sure Ivy is getting an earful across the hall. The walls aren't soundproof, unlike the basement. There's a reason the prison is two floors below where Karina and my son are being kept.

"In case you've forgotten, the Bianchis are still after you."

I hate it as much as she does, forcing her to be under lock and key. But Dorian will have her killed the first chance he gets. And since we tortured and killed Matteo, he'll want revenge.

It's inevitable.

And I have to protect my *Micetta*, even if she thinks she doesn't need protecting. She's wrong.

She opens her mouth to say something, but nothing comes out.

"Cat got your tongue?" I've never seen her speechless. Well, I can't recall it. She always has a comeback, a smart-ass remark to goad me on. She likes to get under my skin and irritate the hell out of me. It's probably why I'm attracted to her.

It's always passionate between us, especially when we're arguing.

"Shut up!"

I laugh under my breath, but she hears me and glances up at me. "Is that all you got?" I give her the chance to counter. To shoot her best shot.

"You showed up at my workplace today and didn't tell me you were coming!"

Is that bad? I did something nice for the kids on her unit. They have cancer. I thought bringing them a few toys would keep their spirits up and bring a little sunshine into their lives.

I'm not great with kids, but I thought I did okay handing them presents. It wasn't something I could majorly fuck up.

"It was supposed to be a surprise. Besides, I thought you'd be happy I was being selfless," I say. "I was trying to show you I'm not the monster you think I am. There's more than one side of me. I'm not just a mafia interrogator."

She rolls her lips tight, pressing them together.

Speechless again.

Twice in one evening.

Victory tastes sweet.

Karina shuffles her feet and glances down at the floor, dejected. She opens her mouth, and I assume she's about to apologize, but a soft puff of air slips out instead.

Maybe she's not good with apologies. It's not like I ever have to apologize. It would be seen as weak, and I'm not the least bit interested in appearing fragile.

"What you did today at the hospital, for those kids, it was very nice," Karina whispers. Her toes nudge the floor as she fidgets and glances up at me after she's done speaking. It's like she's waiting for me to give her something back.

"I'm glad you appreciated the gesture, and next time I want to do something, I won't be quite so secretive."

"Thank you." Her words hang in the air as she stares at me. Her eyes are heavy.

There's a brokenness to her that pulls at my heart.

"I'm sorry," she whispers. Her tongue darts out and swipes across her lips. "I shouldn't have run. I was doing what I thought was best for my son."

"Our son," I correct her. He's as much my child as he is hers. Maybe I didn't raise him for the first few years, but that was only because she didn't tell me about him.

I would have been there for my kid from the moment I found out she was pregnant. I may not have been happy about the news, but I wouldn't have abandoned her or the kid.

"Do you understand why it's imperative that you stay here with Ashton?" I want her to know that I'm not keeping her here, locked up, because I want to. It's out of need and necessity. She and my son's safety take priority over their freedom.

It's not as though I don't take him to private school daily and make sure that he's inside the building before I leave. And when the school day ends, I'm right there to pick him up and bring him back home with me.

Karina nods. "Will you ever be able to stop the Bianchis?" she asks. "That man in the prison, did he help you?"

"We've been feuding for a long time, but we're getting close." I can't elaborate. It's not safe for her to know the details. Matteo did give us a wealth of knowledge in his last few moments.

I pull her to sit beside me on the bed, my hand gripping her wrist. Slowly, I draw my thumb in light circles against her soft skin. "How about I take you out Friday night?"

"Like a date?" her voice squeaks.

Is she nervous?

We're married. There are plenty of opportunities for dates and other things. I have the rest of my life to woo Karina and convince her that I want to be married to her. Maybe it happened out of desperation and the need to save her life, but my desire isn't any less real.

"Is that a problem?" I ask.

She tugs on her bottom lip. "Does that mean we get to leave the house?"

I can't help but chuckle. Is that all she's thinking about?

Escaping.

"Yes, but Ashton stays behind. Ivy can babysit him." While I don't like or trust Ivy, Karina trusts her sister, and I believe Ivy wouldn't hurt a hair on Ashton's head. That's good enough for me.

Plus, if Ashton is at the house, Karina won't try to escape. After our date, she'll want to return home to be with her son.

"I can work with that," Karina whispers.

Reaching for her jaw, I stroke her soft, supple skin with the pads of my fingers. "Do not fear me, *Micetta*."

Her breathing hitches, and she gives the faintest nod. A slight blush spreads across her cheeks and down the dip of her shirt toward her cleavage.

I try not to stare, but I'm not a gentleman. The redness makes her even sexier, whether she realizes it or not.

Her ruby lips part, and it takes all my strength not to run my thumb over them.

"I'm not afraid of you," Karina whispers.

"Good, because I would never hurt you." She should know all that I'm doing to protect her. There would be no reason to harm my wife.

It's a strange notion that I'm married. I stare at her lips, refraining from leaning in and taking a taste. My breathing deepens, matching hers.

"Is it warm in here?" Karina asks.

Yes, it feels like the sun is baking me. "There's a way to fix that little problem," I say with a smirk. "You have too many clothes on."

She snorts. "Wow. Your mind went right for the gutter."

"Mine?" Karina is mouthy. I like it. I want to cover her lips with mine, but I refrain. "Your face looks sunburned. Did I stoke a fire?"

"It's anger."

I lean in and brush my lips across her cheek. "If you say so, *Micetta*," I whisper, brushing her hair behind her ear.

She shivers from my touch. "You didn't feel that."

Grinning, I kiss a soft path along her ear to her jaw, leading to her mouth. But I don't give in to temptation. I drag the moment out. I want her to lean in. I want Karina to take control and kiss me. I can feel her desire, the pull of electricity between us. I'm teasing her, but I want her to be the one to feel she has the power.

"Feel what?" I mumble between kisses.

She groans and throws her hand up to her forehead.

"Feverish?" I tease.

She falls back onto the mattress. "Something like that," she rasps. Karina is already gasping for air.

The rise and fall of her chest, watching her out of breath because of a few kisses, is highly arousing.

She wants me.

## 38

## KARINA

I barely slept, tossing and turning, thinking about my upcoming date with Aurielo. Why do I feel like a teenage girl?

We're married.

It shouldn't be that big a deal that he's taking me out. But the only time I've been allowed anywhere is to work. Otherwise, I've been sequestered upstairs to either my bedroom or Ashton's.

"I can't believe you're actually going to go out to dinner with him," Ivy says.

I don't think it's jealousy, mostly anger in her tone.

"He's not that bad of a guy," I say, pulling her across the room to talk away from Ashton. He's coloring in his brand-new dinosaur coloring book that Aurielo brought home this afternoon for him.

Aurielo has been trying. Since the moment he found out I had a kid, he wanted to be there for him. Before he even knew Ashton was his own flesh and blood.

What kind of savage would do that?

"He's in the mafia, and he forced you to marry him!" Ivy scolds me.

Like I forgot why I'm here. I roll my eyes and fold my arms across my chest. "He saved my life, and I agreed to this life. His boss ordered him to execute me."

"He doesn't have to take orders from him," Ivy says. "He could have stood up to him."

"The mob boss? Are you serious?" I ask.

Alessandro scares me. The way he carries himself, I worry if I give him a dirty look unintentionally, he'll pull out his gun and kill me on the spot. He's not a man to have regrets.

Maybe I was wrong about Aurielo.

He's been kind to Ashton, teaching him to play catch. Every weekday, he drives him to private school and picks him up. Not to mention, he foots the bill for private education. Plus, he's an attentive father.

"I need to get ready," I say. I don't want to argue with Ivy. I love my sister, but we've never seen eye-to-eye. We are identical only in looks. That's how it's always been.

I open the bedroom door and step into the hallway. Giovan is standing guard. "Making sure I don't run?" I offer a smile.

He doesn't look the least bit amused.

I point to my bedroom. "I'm just going to get dressed for tonight," I say.

Stalking across the hall, I head into the bedroom and flip the light. The bed is already made, not a surprise, but the giant white box on the bed has me curious. There's a folded note attached to the lid.

*For Karina.*

It's simple and to the point.

At least I know I'm allowed to open the box, and I'm not snooping. I remove the lid and am stunned by the bold red dress. It's beautiful and soft under my touch. I lift the dress by the spaghetti straps and hold it up to my body.

Another note falls to the floor that was tucked inside the box.

*To match your blush.*

Smiling, I shake my head. I guess he wants me to wear this tonight, which is good since I don't have anything fancy for a date.

I gather the dress and head into the shower to get ready before dinner. I want to wow Aurielo, especially since he picked out the dress.

When did he have time to do that? While I was at work today?

———

We arrive at the restaurant and promptly are escorted to our table. It's a small private table in the busy restaurant. The lights are dimmed, the atmosphere romantic.

He pulls out the chair for me to sit. "You look absolutely stunning," Aurielo whispers into my ear.

I'm sure my blush matches the gown. That was his intent, wasn't it? "Thank you," I say. "You clean up really well yourself."

It sounds stupid coming from my lips. He's always in a fancy suit for work, but he looks sharper, cleaner, sexier tonight. I don't know what it is, but I want to jump him.

The hostess hands us each a menu before disappearing to seat another guest.

I glance over at the menu. The prices are insane. "Have you eaten here before?"

"A few times," Aurielo says. "Everything I've had is always delicious."

He gestures the waitress over and orders a bottle of red wine, along with several appetizers.

That sounds fine to me. I can't imagine having room for dinner after appetizers.

The waitress heads back to put in the order and bring out the wine.

"I hope you're hungry," Aurielo says.

I'm starving. "Everything smells so good," I admit. "And it all sounds wonderful." It's been a while since I've eaten out. I can't even remember when I went to a fancy restaurant last.

"Did you see anything that you want to try on the menu?" Aurielo asks.

The waitress brings over a bottle of red and three glasses. She uncorks the bottle and hands the cork to Aurielo.

I assume it's to smell. I have no clue what the hell she's doing. I've never ordered a full bottle of wine at a restaurant. It's too expensive, and I don't typically drink that much. But Ivy does, and if I order a bottle with my sister, then she'll get trashed.

The waitress pours a small amount into the glass for Aurielo to try.

He swirls the wine and breathes in the aroma before having a taste.

"How is it, sir?" the waitress asks.

"Very good," Aurielo says. "You can pour us each a glass."

The waitress pours a new glass for Aurielo and a second for me before hurrying to help another table.

I feel out of sorts at such a fancy restaurant, but Aurielo fits right in. Is this his lifestyle? How he lives? Lavishly? Does he come here with his mafia buddies?

"What do you think?" he asks as I take a sip of wine. I haven't eaten since lunch and don't want to get tipsy too early into the night.

"It's good, but I don't know much about wine," I confess. "But it is the best bottle I've ever had."

He smiles proudly. "Good."

I don't dare ask how much it costs.

"Did you find anything on the menu for dinner?" he asks again. I never answered him earlier when the waitress interrupted us with the wine unveiling.

"It all looks really good."

"How about I order a few dishes that we can share?" Aurielo suggests.

I like the sound of that, but it seems like a lot of food. "Are you sure we need that much food? You ordered a bunch of appetizers already!" We'll have leftovers for a week, even with feeding everyone back at the mansion.

"The portions here are pretty small. Delicious, but you'll be glad we ordered so many foods to try."

I don't argue. Aurielo seems to know what he's talking about. He's been here before.

When the waitress resurfaces, Aurielo orders for both of us, picking four meals off the menu. It seems a little excessive, especially with the appetizers already ordered, but I'm starving.

I sip my wine, enjoying the sweet taste on my tongue. It's tart but not bitter, leaving no dry aftertaste. It's good wine. I'm used to the five-dollar bottles at the grocery store. This wine wasn't down the cheap aisle.

"It's good, isn't it?" Aurielo says.

"You know your wines." I give him credit where it's due. "Do you and the guys drink a lot?"

Aurielo chuckles. "Yes, but not typically wine. I save that for special occasions."

My mouth is dry. I reach for the wine, taking another taste. "This is a special occasion?" I squeak.

Aurielo reaches for the bottle and fills my glass, not waiting for the waitress to return. She's busy, and he seems intent on keeping me drinking. Maybe he wants to make sure we both have a good time and are relaxed.

I don't know how we're driving home tonight. But he's still on his first glass, and I'm not.

"I'd consider our first real date a special occasion," Aurielo says. "Funny how we do everything backward."

He isn't wrong. I smile at his remark. "Yeah, this isn't how I saw my life going." I don't mean it in a bad way. It's just all a surprise. It still feels unreal, but I'm settling into what we have.

A woman with six-inch stilettos approaches our table. She's a platinum blonde. Obviously dyed. Her makeup is a little over the top, and her dress is two sizes too tight, and she's sporting a pregnant belly. "Aurielo?"

Shit.

Do they know each other?

The smile disappears from his face. "Etta, what are you doing here?" He glances at her belly, which is practically in his face as he's still seated.

"Having dinner with my father." She points with her perfectly manicured fingernails across the restaurant at Dorian Bianchi.

My stomach flops.

The appetite I had for dinner vanishes. This is Etta Bianchi, the don's daughter.

Wasn't there something between Etta and Aurielo?

His body language is rigid and stiff. She's practically sitting in his lap as she runs her fingers through his hair. "In case you're wondering," Etta says and glances at me. "The baby is his."

I wasn't wondering. It didn't even cross my mind.

Now I can't help but feel sick.

Bile rises to my throat. I reach for my wine glass and finish the liquid. I should have reached for my water glass, but I needed something to dull the growing ache in my chest.

"I'm not the only man you slept with," Aurielo says. "Show me a paternity test."

Etta pouts, turning up the drama and waterworks. Her eyes glisten with tears. The girl could have been an actress, though she isn't a good one. Just overly dramatic. She's the kind of girlfriend you run away from the first chance you get.

"Do you see what I have to deal with?" Etta says, glancing at me. "He'll grow bored with you and your son, just like he did me. Don't expect him to be a real father." She runs her fingers through his hair again.

Aurielo grabs her wrist, stopping her from further touching him. "That's enough," he growls.

I can't take any more of this woman. I stand.

Aurielo's eyes widen. He must think I'm leaving.

The grin on Etta's face grows wider, believing that she has won.

She's dead wrong.

"I'm his wife," I say proudly before I close the gap and lean down, shoving my mouth forcefully over Aurielo's lips.

Etta takes a step back and clears her throat. Maybe she's waiting for the kiss to end and for him to say something.

I don't stop kissing Aurielo, and he reciprocates hungrily.

He pulls me into his lap.

I wrap my arms around his neck, deepening the kiss, if that's at all possible. The world around us disappears, although I know in the back of my head that Etta is out there watching. I don't care. Let her watch. Let her talk.

Sitting on Aurielo's lap, I feel his body react and stir awake.

A grin spreads across my lips. Panting, I pull back slightly to catch my breath. My heart is slamming against my ribcage.

Aurielo's eyes are on me and me alone.

# 39

# AURIELO

That kiss. Damn. Talk about sparks flying.

I had no idea Karina had a jealous streak inside her.

I'm proud of Karina, standing up to Etta. Not many women would do that, especially to the don's family. Etta is practically a mafia princess. She's a spoiled rich kid who never changed. Just got older.

One day Etta will run her family's empire. She's the heir to the Bianchi fortune. And merging our families together would end the war.

But I never loved Etta. And her wandering eye only secured the fact that I would be second to her, if not third.

I don't come in second, ever.

With Karina, the tension between us is different. It's hotter. Wilder. She's spicy and raw, without a cruel bone in her body. There's a toughness to Karina that's sexy, but an innocence that makes my cock hard with one look at her.

Etta has retreated with her head hung. She's not used to being rejected.

Karina never has to worry about me rejecting her, cheating on her, or frankly, even wanting to look at another woman. The fire that burns bright is solely for her.

The kiss made me realize what I've been missing, the passion and desire. There was never anything more than ravishing sex with Etta.

While Karina and I haven't exactly opened up entirely to one another, I believe we still can. There's hope for a future with us together. And not just because we're wed.

Her fingers run through my hair, making my head foggy with wanton thoughts as our lips are fused together again—this time, the kiss isn't fueled by jealousy or rage on her part. Etta has disappeared across the restaurant.

"I truly am sorry, Aurielo," Karina whispers. She leans her forehead against mine. My heart pitter-patters in my chest. The way she stares at me and says my name makes my stomach somersault.

I've never been in love, but if this is what the first stirrings of butterflies feel like, I'm terrified of what falling head over heels will mean.

"What for?" I ask, pulling back just slightly. My stomach does a flop. She's not going to suggest leaving with Ashton, is she? I can't take the thought of being away from my family.

Her fingers run along the nape of my neck. Her touch is soft and gentle, soothing as she caresses my skin. "I was scared. Terrified after the man pointed a gun at you, at me," she whispers. "I thought running away with Ashton was the right choice, but he's your son."

"Do you still think I'm a monster?" I'm afraid of the answer that she'll give me, but I ask, nonetheless.

"You do things that I don't agree with," Karina says. She doesn't hide her disappointment at what I do. It's a part of who I am, and she has to know that I'd never hurt her or our son. "But your love for Ashton is real. I trust that you won't let him become a villain when he grows up."

A smile tugs at the corners of my lips. "Is that what you think of me? That I'm a villain?" I've murdered men, but not out of desire.

Necessity.

The waitress brings our food to the table, and Karina climbs off my lap and returns to her chair seated across from me. Already, I miss her warmth, the feel of her fingers against my scalp and in my hair. My lips still tingle from when we kissed moments ago.

"Everything looks good," Karina whispers, reaching for her cloth napkin to put on her lap.

I'm hungry for dessert, but it will have to wait until we get home. The sooner, the better.

———

After we finish dinner, the drive back to the house takes forever. My hand is in hers, keeping her close, our fingers tangling together while I keep my other hand on the steering wheel.

My attention is mostly focused on the road.

"I had fun tonight. Thank you for taking me out," Karina whispers. Her voice is soft, fragile. She's staring at me.

I cast a quick glance and smile in her direction but return my attention to the road. It's dark and late. There are a few drivers on the road already, and I've had enough wine to know any more, and I'd have had trouble staying in my lane.

It's hard enough to keep my attention on the street and not the sexy little vixen seated beside me. My cock twitches in my trousers.

While I want Karina desperately, I don't know what will happen after we graze the front entrance.

Will she grow cold and distant? She hasn't asked me about Etta and her pregnancy. She inevitably will, and I have no reason to lie to her.

"It was a nice night, even with all the unnecessary drama," I say, glancing at her briefly.

"Your ex-girlfriend is something else." Karina sighs and untangles her hand from mine. "Is it true the baby she's pregnant with might be yours?"

"Mine or half a dozen other guys she slept with," I say. "I'm not the only one who climbed into her bed."

"You don't know without a doubt that she slept with other men."

I do. Etta had another man in the shower with her when I came over unannounced. "She fucked at least one guy in the shower when I showed up. And given the time and how far along she is, it could just as easily be his baby."

Karina presses her lips together. "Are you going to insist on a paternity test?"

"If it's my child, then yes, I'd like to be a part of his or her life. But being tied to Etta for the rest of my life, it's a lot to deal with," I say.

Karina exhales a heavy sigh. "When were you planning on telling me about this? I should be part of the decision."

"Why?"

"I'm your wife! It's not something that you should be keeping from me. If there's going to be a second kid around, I ought to know about it."

I glance at Karina.

She's biting her bottom lip, tugging it between her teeth. Her breathing is louder, more anxious.

"What's wrong?"

"Dorian threatened my son and me, I'm not sure it'll ever be over. Especially if Etta is carrying your child." Karina runs a hand through her hair. Her breathing increases again, each breath louder and more pronounced.

Is she having a panic attack or bad anxiety? I've never witnessed anyone hyperventilate, even in all my interrogations, but Karina is struggling to breathe.

I rest a hand on her thigh and pull over, flipping the hazard lights on.

"Just breathe," I coax, encouraging her to take slower breaths and calm herself down. My hands rest on her thighs, gently rubbing back and forth in soothing motions to help her settle.

Eventually, her breathing returns to a much more normal pace.

"I understand you're scared," I say. I don't want to minimize what she's going through. "But I swear on my life that I will do everything to protect our son and you."

Several seconds of silence fall over the vehicle. I return my attention back to the road and pull out into traffic.

Her breathing is calmer, more peaceful. "I know you will. I trust you," she whispers.

A few days ago, I wouldn't have known if she meant it, but right now, I do. I trust her, too.

Karina's voice is soft, calm. "What are we going to do about him?"

"Who?" I ask.

"Dorian. The man who threatened your son's life. You can't just wait for him to come after us."

She's right. More than I'd like to admit. "You're okay with what that means?" I ask, glancing at her out of the corner of my eye.

"I'm not happy about it, but I don't want him coming after Ashton," Karina says. She presses her lips tight, her brow furrowed.

"What?" I ask.

"Will Etta come after us if we order a hit on her family? You said he's like a father to her."

Yes, inevitably, that is what happens unless we take down their entire organization. "Don't worry about Etta."

"How can I not worry about her?" Her voice raises an octave.

"She stands to inherit everything. While she'll hate us for killing him, I know Etta well enough to know that she'll be glad he's dead."

"Why?"

"She's ready to take over the business. Etta isn't ruthless enough to kill her own flesh and blood." I hope I'm right and that she doesn't take vengeance on us for murdering him.

He's not an innocent man, Don Bianchi.

Etta never wanted to marry me or anyone else. It had been at Dorian's insistence that we join ranks together, command the entire city as one faction.

I suspected that he didn't trust that Etta could handle the task on her own and, while he was alive, wanted to bask in the wealth and glory that he could by merging our enterprises.

Except Don Rinaldi doesn't trust Don Bianchi, and neither do I.

Alliances get betrayed. It happens every day. We're careful who we allow inside our world. Traitors can take on various shapes and sizes.

"I hope you're right," Karina says, her voice soft and timid. She clears her throat, her tone much clearer and louder. "I won't leave my son without a father."

## 40

# KARINA

"And if Etta is the new don, what does that mean for the child she's carrying? If it's yours?" I ask.

He's already told me that he wants to be a part of his son or daughter's life, but I can't see how that would be possible, especially if the Rinaldis kill Don Bianchi.

Aurielo parks out front and shuts off the engine. He doesn't step out of the car. He turns to face me.

"I'll probably never see the kid," he says. "Unless there are long, drawn-out court battles, and even then, she'll try to destroy my reputation. I'm sure she'll fight for full custody."

"And that's assuming she hasn't bought the judge," I say.

"Yeah, that's highly possible too," Aurielo mutters under his breath. He opens the car door, and I do the same.

A moment later, he's at my side, offering me his arm as he escorts me back inside the mansion.

But this time, I don't feel imprisoned. I feel safe at home.

His hand falls to the small of my back as we head in through the main doors. "Do you want anything to drink? A snack?" Aurielo asks.

I slip out of my shoes and leave them by the door.

"I can't eat another bite." It was amazing to me how much food he ordered and that we managed to eat all of it. Aurielo was right. The portions were tiny. I glance at the stairs. "I want to check on Ashton. Tuck him into bed."

"All right," he says.

I head quietly up the staircase. It's nearing midnight, and I don't know how many people are awake, but I don't want to be the cause. I'm quiet when I approach the bedroom door. Giovan is stationed outside the door.

Is he preventing Ivy from leaving or guarding Ashton?

I sneak into their bedroom and give Ashton a kiss goodnight.

Ivy stirs, rolling around on the cot. The metal squeaking as she shifts. "You're home," she says. Her eyes open lazily, but she still looks tired. "How was your date?"

"We can talk about it more tomorrow." I have the day off and don't want to keep her up or wake Ashton. I bend down and kiss her cheek. "Thanks for looking after Ash."

"No problem," she says with a muffled yawn. "Where else would I go?"

I laugh under my breath. "Go back to sleep." I ease myself out of their bedroom and across the hall.

Aurielo is already in the shower. There's a trail of his clothes on the floor. Can't he pick up after himself?

I don't clean up after him. I glance from the dresser to the bathroom.

Oh, fuck it. Tonight went really well.

I don't want it to be over.

I sneak into the bathroom. The shower is running, and the curtain is closed.

"Karina?" Aurielo asks.

"I guess I'm not good at sneaking in," I confess as I strip out of my dress. I didn't wear any panties, but he didn't get the opportunity to discover that small secret. Maybe next time.

There will be a next time. Won't there?

I need to make certain, especially if there's any chance that Etta's carrying his child. I don't want any second thoughts running through his head that he should have chosen her, married her, been with her.

He's mine, and I want him to know that I appreciate what he did tonight.

I tug my bottom lip between my teeth. Just thinking about that kiss at the restaurant has me antsy. His kiss had been more passionate than any other kiss that we'd shared. There'd been something raw and primal that I'd never felt before.

I want more.

I pull back the curtain and climb into the shower.

Aurielo yanks the curtain closed behind me. He grabs me by the waist, pulling me with him under the spray, his lips crushing mine.

I'm hungry for him. Desire builds inside of me. I can't explain how I can fear him, hate him, and want to fuck him all within a short span of time.

He drives me crazy.

"Fuck, you're wet," he mumbles against my lips, his fingers gliding down between my folds.

"Isn't that the point?" I rasp. We are in the shower. Or did he already forget?

My mind is in a fog. His fingers stroke me, teasing my lips apart, making me ready to beg for more. I don't want slow and drawn out. I can't do that tonight. Need outweighs everything else.

And I need him.

He must sense my urgency as I moan at his rough touch. My insides throb for release, the pulsating building, and he hasn't even fucked me yet.

Aurielo lifts me in his arms, and my legs wrap around his hips as he enters me. He's rough and hard. It's exactly what I need tonight.

I gasp as he fills me.

My eyes slam shut. My back is pressed against the cold tile of the shower wall, and I shiver. But I don't care. All I feel is warmth flowing through my body, heat building and burning inside of me, begging to break free.

His mouth claims my neck, marking me as he sucks against my skin.

I don't try to hide my moans. Every thrust makes my core ache in the most delirious way possible. The steam from the shower heats up the bathroom as Aurielo pounds into me.

Our bodies are slick with sweat and water from the shower.

I pull him tighter, harder, closer, wanting to be one with him.

Digging my fingernails into his back, I claw at him, pulling him deeper.

He grunts his satisfaction, kissing and sucking my skin. "Come for me, *Micetta*," he whispers into my ear.

Aurielo nips my earlobe, and I tighten onto him, feeling the first slight shudder. His words coax me closer.

His lips move to my mouth, covering mine, silencing my moans as I grow closer toward oblivion. My insides throb and ache, the pulsating sensation overwhelming as my toes curl and I tighten my hold on Aurielo.

I tremble in his embrace and clench down as he continues thrusting, grunting, letting go with me.

My heart pounds wildly against my ribcage.

His forehead rests against mine, together, panting, gasping for breath. My legs feel like rubber when I stand.

He traps me for a few seconds, brushing a strand of hair behind my ear. "Breathe," he whispers, pinning me with his gaze.

That's what I'm trying to do, but the bathroom is stifling.

He keeps me held against the shower wall, my back enjoying the slight cool chill from the tile. He shuts off the shower and sweeps me up in his arms.

"What are you doing?" I laugh.

"Carrying you to bed."

I smirk, wrapping my arms around his neck. "Never took you for the romantic type."

"Don't tell anyone, or I'll have to deny it."

# 41

## AURIELO

I should be on the team taking out Dorian Bianchi, but that's the job of a soldier, not an interrogator. If they bring back any men alive, I'll have my chance to interrogate them, but that isn't the plan.

They are going in to execute Dorian on Alessandro's orders.

It wasn't hard to convince Alessandro to go to war with the Bianchis. We've been battling them for as long as I can remember. Sending in soldiers to attack isn't an easy game. It involves planning, infiltrating, and managing to escape.

It's the first time I'm both grateful and upset not to be a soldier. I want to be on the inside and be part of the crew that takes him out. But I also would rather stay back to protect my family. Someone has to stay at the compound.

Although I'm not exactly at the house. Karina is with me. We're picking up Ashton from school.

My hand clenches around hers as we walk from the parked car to the front, gated entrance. The school will be letting out any minute.

The strike on the Bianchi compound is happening simultaneously, and while the men have their orders not to harm Etta, casualties of war happen. I wait for their call to find out the news.

"I can't believe I have a day off in forever and it was spent cooped up at the mansion," Karina says.

I raise an eyebrow, glancing at her. "We didn't waste the day," I say. We spent the early afternoon with Ivy, helping her move into her new bedroom down the hallway. Alessandro agreed to give her a room of her own, and after Dorian is dead, she'll be allowed to leave the compound with a bodyguard.

Maybe if she wasn't Karina's identical twin, we could let her live on her own, but looking like Karina, being her sister, puts both girls at risk.

Even if the soldiers kill Dorian, we've made too many enemies.

"I'm sure Ivy is appreciative that she doesn't have to share a room with her nephew anymore," Karina says.

"I should hope so. I had to pull quite a few strings to convince Alessandro to give up another bedroom."

Karina snorts. "The mansion has a thousand rooms. He can't spare one more?"

"A thousand?" I shoot a glance at her. She's exaggerating.

"Okay, a hundred."

She's cute, and if it wasn't for that wicked grin, I'd remind her that Alessandro has always been good to me, protected me. But she has a way of making me lose my thoughts. I want to kiss her and lean in, but the school bell tolls, and the doors open.

We sign Ashton out and head toward the car.

"Daddy," Ashton says, glancing at me over his shoulder. "Can I spend the night at Ryan's house? He invited me to sleep over this Friday."

Did I hear him correctly?

Daddy?

I freeze, and Karina squeezes my hand. "We haven't met Ryan's parents yet," she says, softening the blow. She must realize the same fears that I have. Who are Ryan's parents? What if they're part of the Bianchi family?

"You can meet them when you drop me off. Please," Ashton whines.

We approach the car, and I open the back door, letting Ashton into the backseat. "How about we talk about it more when we get home?" There's no way that I'm letting him spend the night at a stranger's house, but maybe we can have his friend over?

The fact he called me Daddy, I can't say no to him. Does he know that?

What are the chances that Alessandro will approve such a request?

None.

Alessandro doesn't have kids. He has no significant other. Just random women he brings home to bed. They never stay the night. They're not invited to come back, either. He's the typical playboy who isn't interested in children.

How many kids has he fathered who he doesn't know exist?

He was our role model, the alpha of the pack.

That was until I met Karina the second time. After discovering what I've been missing, I've never want to return to that life. The emptiness and loneliness consumed me.

————

Returning to the house, we head outside into the garden. It's a nice day. I want Ashton to enjoy the warmth and sunlight in the last few days of autumn before winter bites.

I hand him a glove that fits his little hand, and we toss a ball between us. It's a good release of energy.

The walkie-talkie secured to my belt has been silent. There's been no communication from Alessandro within the compound or the guards standing at the gate.

My attention is on Ashton. I want him to remember this moment with his father playing ball with him.

There are guards posted outside the compound and several still onsite, but I can't help but worry that the Bianchis might retaliate.

We did kill their second in command and are going in to take down their don. If our soldiers get slaughtered, and it's a setup, then, any moment, Bianchi's soldiers could come tearing down the fort, destroying our home.

Maybe I should have taken Ashton and Karina out of the city for the day. But I'm not a man to run.

I don't cower or hide.

I wait.

And the best way to do that is to spend time with Ashton. He's the perfect distraction. A moment to both bond with the boy, my son, and forget the horror that's happening outside the compound.

The crackle of static on the walkie-talkie jars my attention. I drop the ball just as Ashton tosses it at my glove. I reach for the device on my belt loop.

"Daddy!" Ashton tries to get my attention.

I turn the sound louder to make sure I hear what's being said.

"Target is neutralized."

I exhale a heavy breath.

"Throw me the ball," Ashton whines and stomps his feet, dragging them across the grass.

The kid has about as much patience as I do—one of the many traits he's inherited from his old man.

I put the walkie-talkie back on the belt clip and grab the ball off the ground. "You want this?" I ask, showing him the ball. It's like a tennis ball, so it shouldn't bust any windows if Ashton misses a catch or overshoots a throw.

"Yes," he groans and stands there with the biggest pout on his ruby lips. The kid is going to be a heartbreaker, no doubt. I just hope he doesn't take after Alessandro, parading women around without a care in the world.

Thankfully, I don't let him near Don Rinaldi, not that the boss wants time with my kid.

I toss the ball back to Ashton, and he throws it at me. The game continues for several minutes, helping ease my mind and the tension pulsing through me. It's hard not to wonder if there were any causalities other than our target, Dorian Bianchi.

The sun is low across the horizon, and Karina wraps her arms around herself. She looks chilled. "One last throw," I say to Ashton.

"Aww," he fusses, giving me a fastball that requires me to outstretch my arm to catch before it breezes past me for the door.

I open the French doors and escort Karina and Ashton inside.

Alessandro stalks down the hallway and pauses, seeing us entering from the garden. "Aurielo, can I have a word with you?" It's not a question.

"Of course. Do you want to take him upstairs? Get him washed up for dinner?" I suggest, handing Karina my glove and ball to take with her.

I smile my thanks, and she escorts Ashton up the staircase.

I wait to make sure they do as instructed before I follow into Alessandro's office.

Is there an interrogation that I'll be required to do tonight? Is that why he asked me to speak with him?

I give a firm knock on the open door before Alessandro gestures me into his office.

"Come in and have a seat."

I shut the door and grab the chair across from his desk. "What's going on?" I ask.

I don't want to consider the possibility that some of our soldiers may not make it home. It's part of the job, putting your life on the line for the family.

He exhales a heavy breath. It takes a moment for him to speak. Is he thinking about what he wants to put into words? He's usually quite direct, blunt, in fact.

"As I'm sure you heard on the radio, Dorian is dead."

I nod and clasp my hands together in front of me on the desk. "Yes, I'm relieved to know that my family is safe." Karina and Ashton are part of that family, the Rinaldis.

His gaze flickers for a brief instant. "There were, unfortunately, a few casualties. It's to be expected in matters of war," Alessandro says.

The air is thick, heavy.

My stomach flops. Is it my younger brother, Giovan? Did something happen to him during the attack? My mouth is dry, parched. I can't speak. It's too hard to form the words aloud.

"I don't know how to tell you this," Alessandro says. His expression is full of remorse. "Etta is dead."

I swallow. There's a lump in my throat that keeps me from speaking. The nausea roiling through doesn't help me focus, either.

"Dead?" I croak. "What about the baby?"

Alessandro shakes his head. "The baby didn't survive, either. I'm sorry. I know that you and Etta were once close, but it had to be done. All ties between the Rinaldis and Bianchis needed to be severed."

I stare at the mahogany desk. My fingers graze the wood lines. They're perfectly polished, but they look rough beneath the surface. Not all is as it seems.

"You ordered the hit on her?" I need to know the truth. I glance up at his intense scrutiny.

"I did," Alessandro says. He holds no regret, no sorrow. Only acceptance that he's won the war.

My vision spins, and I take a calm, steady breath to focus. I open my mouth, but Alessandro speaks before I have time to say anything.

"Consider your words carefully, Aurielo. You have a family here, a wife and son, with our protection, and a job that pays handsomely. Etta was a distraction that would have weaseled her way into our home and our lives. I couldn't let that happen."

"She could have been carrying my child," I seethe.

Alessandro gives a mere shrug. "That is a possibility that I considered, but what would you have done? Shared custody with her? She would have run the entire Bianchi empire and would have destroyed what you have with that woman upstairs." He holds up his finger to silence me. "While you might not have married Karina out of love, I see the way you look at that boy, like he's your own flesh and blood. Don't lose focus of the bigger picture."

"Which is?" I rasp. My heart pounds wildly against my chest. The room is stifling, and my stomach won't stop somersaulting.

Etta is dead, and this is supposed to be a good thing?

I understand his position as don, his reasoning for what he did, but I should have been consulted before, not after her death.

"Your family needs you, Aurielo. The Rinaldis need you."

There's nothing more to say. At least not today. I understand the game. Alessandro took out the enemy and the next in line for the throne. It was a strategic decision for several reasons. He didn't have to consult me. He didn't even have to tell me himself, but he did.

Maybe I should be grateful for his honesty.

"Am I dismissed?" I ask.

There's nothing more for me to say.

Alessandro nods and gestures for me to leave.

I head out of his office, leaving the door open before finding my way upstairs. "They're in Ivy's room," Francesco says.

"Thanks." I head down the hall for Ivy's bedroom and give a brief knock on the door before entering.

Inside the room, there's a giant canvas tarp laid out and an open can of lavender paint.

"Does Alessandro know what you're doing?" I can't imagine he gave them permission to paint any room in the mansion, let alone purple!

"Relax," Ivy says with a giggle. "He told me I could do whatever I wanted to the room."

"And that includes painting it?" He just had Etta executed. While I doubt he considers Ivy a threat, it still makes me nervous.

"Big scary guard in the hallway bought me the paint. So, I'm pretty sure it's allowed," Ivy says. "Chill out."

Karina stalks across the room and wraps her arms around my waist. "Do you think we can convince the big scary don to let us paint our bedroom pink?"

"Hell no." She'd better be joking. There's no way in hell I'm sleeping in a pink bedroom.

"Can I paint mine too?" Ashton quips.

Karina drops a kiss to my cheek before glancing at her son and untangling herself from my embrace. She bends down to our son's eye level. "Of course, Ash. What color do you want your bedroom to be?"

I groan.

How am I supposed to tell Ashton no?

Did Alessandro give Ivy permission to paint her bedroom purple? My stomach does somersaults. It sounds completely out of character. Crazy. Insane.

Wait.

Are they sleeping together?

No, that couldn't be. I mean, when? Ivy has been crashing in Ashton's room for days. And besides, Ivy and Karina are identical twins. I grimace at the thought. I swear if he so much as touched Ivy, I'll kill him myself.

"You and Alessandro aren't—" I can't finish the sentence. Bile rises to my throat just considering the disgusting notion that the two of them might have done something intimate together.

"What?" Ivy glances at me, a scowl on her face, purple-dipped paintbrush in hand.

"Sleeping together?" I cringe at my own words.

Ivy rolls her eyes. "Not that it's any of your business, but no, he's not my type."

To say I'm relieved, is an understatement. "Fair enough." I don't ask her what her type is and if she's sleeping with one of the guards. I don't want to know about it. For the first time since I've met her, though, she seems happy.

Ashton grabs a roller and dips it into the plastic tray on the canvas. He doesn't even try to wipe down any of the paint before smacking the wall with it, the paint dripping everywhere, making a huge mess.

Ivy grabs the roller from Ashton and fixes the disaster before it ends up everywhere but the wall. She glances over her shoulder at me. "If you both want to help, maybe get changed into something else?"

I glance at Karina and gesture for her to follow me out of Ivy's bedroom. I want a few minutes with her alone anyhow. This gives me the perfect excuse to steal a moment of her time.

## 42

## KARINA

"What's going on?" I ask. It's easy to sense when something isn't quite right.

Aurielo blew through the door. I thought he was going to take it down when he came into Ivy's bedroom. I doubt it was about the paint job.

He opens the bedroom door, and I step in first. He shuts it behind himself and begins to strip out of his clothes, heading for the dresser to find something to wear that can get paint on it.

My gaze moves over his body. He's never been shy about the way he looks. He's hot; there's no reason for him to have any self-doubt, but his confidence is just as sexy as he is.

"Alessandro called me into his office."

I already knew that small tidbit. "And?" I'm waiting for the juicy parts of the story if he's willing to divulge it to me.

"Etta is dead."

His expression is empty. The smile from moments earlier has vanished.

"I'm sorry," I say and step closer, pulling him in for a hug. While I didn't like the woman, the fact that she might have been carrying his child couldn't have been easy for him.

I don't ask for the details. I'm not sure whether he knows them or not, but it's none of my business. If Aurielo wants to tell me what he knows, he will when he's ready.

He nuzzles my neck, and his arms wrap around me, clinging to my body. There's a warmth and comfort in sharing an embrace.

"I love you," I whisper.

I need him to know how I feel. Maybe it isn't the best time to tell him that he's stirred a desire locked up inside of me that I didn't know existed, but a world without him isn't one I want to live in.

His lips crush mine.

My fingers claw through his hair, pulling him tighter as we kiss.

There's a wild hunger, a yearning for more that can't be sated from just a kiss. He pulls back long enough to undo the buckle on his pants.

"Do you think they'll miss us?" I ask.

"Who?" His brow knits in confusion.

"My sister and Ash," I say before leaning in for another taste. The fire has been fueled, and I'm not ready to let go.

# EPILOGUE
## KARINA

Fuck it. How can I be late? We've only had sex a handful of times, and every time we've used a condom.

Except the time in the shower.

But I couldn't be pregnant from that one time. I mean, it wasn't that long ago. Surely, I'd have symptoms. I'd know if I was pregnant. Wouldn't I?

I can't remember the last time I had my period, and buying a pregnancy test isn't the easiest task with a bodyguard constantly over my shoulder.

There are no secrets in the Rinaldi family.

I had to beg Jocelyn to snatch one for me at work, and I snuck it home in my purse. I swore I'd take the test first thing tomorrow morning.

Which is today.

Staring at the double lines, my stomach flops.

At least this time, I'm married.

"Karina?" Aurielo's voice resonates through the bathroom door.

"Ugh, just a sec!" I call and flush the toilet. I'm not ready for a second kid. At least this time, I'm not alone, but it doesn't make me any less nervous.

When I don't appear quick enough, he gives a firm knock. "I'm coming in."

I'm not sure what he's expecting to find, that I've fallen in the toilet? I'm not a toddler potty training.

"Everything okay?" Aurielo asks. "You were taking a while." His eyes land on the pregnancy test on the bathroom counter. "Is that—"

"Yes," I whisper, pressing my lips together. I'm not sure how he'll react, if he'll blame me or be relieved.

It wasn't long ago that he lost Etta, and whether she was pregnant with his child or not, that thought still must be in his head, wondering what if?

He inches closer, glancing down at the double pink lines. "Two lines. Pregnant?" he asks.

"You mean you've never peed on a pregnancy test?" I ask with a laugh. I'm trying to make light of the situation. Maybe we're married, but it isn't like we have a conventional marriage. Having more kids isn't a topic that we've discussed together.

We certainly didn't plan for a pregnancy.

"Sure, but it's never shown two lines," Aurielo teases. He pulls me against him, his hands around the small of my back, his eyes on me. "Tell me what you're thinking, feeling. I want to know everything."

"I'm wondering how this happened," I say.

"Well, do you need a sex-ed lesson?" He chuckles. "Because I thought you knew where babies come from."

I snort and shake my head. "How did this happen?" I ask, wrapping my arms around his neck. I thought we'd been careful. Although, obviously, not careful enough.

He looks distant for a long moment.

"It's yours, in case you're wondering." I don't want him thinking that there's anyone else. There's not even the slightest chance it could be another man's baby.

"I wasn't, but thank you for being faithful," he quips and presses a soft kiss to my lips. "The condom a few weeks ago, it broke."

"What? You didn't think to tell me that?" I untangle from his embrace. Why is he telling me now? Out of guilt? Regret?

"I meant to, but you fell asleep, and then things happened and I forgot."

I roll my lips between my teeth. I'm contemplating a dozen different things I could say, but does it matter? We're married. I love him, and we're pregnant.

Exhaling a soft breath, I stare up into his stern gaze. "You can tell Alessandro that our family is expanding."

It's not a conversation that I want to have with the don.

Aurielo groans and throws his head back, staring up at the ceiling.

He clearly doesn't want to, either. "Oh, come on, you're not carrying the kid for nine months and pushing it out of you. The least you can do is talk with Alessandro and convince him to gift us with another bedroom."

Aurielo pins me with his stare. "And how do you think that's going to go?"

"I don't know. You're a pretty persuasive guy. I think you can handle it," I say and lean in, planting a kiss on his lips. "Good luck, babe."

———

Thank you for reading Savage Vow. Continue the adventure with Unwilling Vow.

**Billionaire seeks surrogate...**

She has a debt to repay and I have a need... for a child.

It is strictly a business transaction, nothing more. After the baby is born, I'll never see her again.

But bringing her into my home is a mistake. It could cost me everything. She's curious. Sassy. And the biggest test to my patience.

How can I handle a child if I can't handle her under my roof? It doesn't help that her hormones are raging and she wants to murder me in my sleep.

I'm not that bad of a guy, I only run the mafia. And she can never find out.

This slow-burn age gap Mafia Romance is a standalone with a happily ever after.

One-click Unwilling Vow now!

**Ready for your next one-click read?** Binge the Eagle Tactical Series starting with Expose: Jaxson.

And sign up for my newsletter to find out about new books, giveaways, and freebies: www.authorwillowfox.com/subscribe

I appreciate your help in spreading the word, including telling a friend. Reviews help readers find books! Please leave a review on your favorite book site.

# GIVEAWAYS, FREE BOOKS, AND MORE GOODIES

I hope you enjoyed Savage Vow and loved Aurielo and Karina's story.

Sign up for my Willow Fox newsletter

If you enjoyed Savage Vow, please take a moment to leave a review. Reviews helps other readers discover my books.

Not sure what to write? That's okay. It doesn't have to be long. You can share how you discovered my book; was it a recommendation by a friend or a book club? Let readers know who your favorite character is or what you'd like to see happen next.

Thank you for reading! I hope you'll consider joining my mailing list for free books, promotions, giveaways, and new release news.

# ABOUT THE AUTHOR

Willow Fox has loved writing since she was in high school (many ages ago). Her small town romances are reflective of living in a small town in rural America.

Whether she's writing romance or sitting outside by the bonfire reading a good book, Willow loves the magic of the written word.

She dreams of being swept off her feet and hopes to do that to her readers!

Visit her website at:

https://authorwillowfox.com

# ALSO BY WILLOW FOX

Eagle Tactical Series

Expose: Jaxson

Stealth: Mason

Conceal: Lincoln

Covert: Jayden

Mafia Marriages

Secret Vow

Captive Vow

Savage Vow

Unwilling Vow

Ruthless Vow

Bratva Brothers

Brutal Boss

Wicked Boss

Possessive Boss

Obsessive Boss

Boxsets

Eagle Tactical Collection

Looking for kinkier books? Try these spicy stories written under the name Allison West.

Boxsets

Academy of Littles

Western Daddies Collection

Obey Daddy Collection

The Alpha Collection

Western Daddies

Her Billionaire Daddy

Her Cowboy Daddy

Her Outlaw Daddy

Her Forbidden Daddy

Standalone Romances

The Victorian Shift

Jailed Little Jade

Prefer a sweeter romance with action and adventure? Check out these titles under the name Ruth Silver.

Aberrant Series

Love Forbidden

Secrets Forbidden

Magic Forbidden

Escape Forbidden

Refuge Forbidden


Boxsets

Gem Apocalypse

Nightblood

Royal Reaper

Royal Deception


Standalones

Stolen Art